McCordsville Elementary
Media Center

# EARTHBORN

Sylvia Waugh

A Dell Yearling Book

Visit us on the Web! www.randomhouse.com/kids

Educators and librarians, for a variety of teaching tools, visit us at
www.randomhouse.com/teachers

ISBN: 0-440-41838-0

Reprinted by arrangement with Delacorte Press

Printed in the United States of America

April 2004

10 9 8 7 6 5 4 3 2 1

OPM

*For my grandson,*

*Liam Peter Waugh*

# Contents

Whatever shape, size, or form you have,
there's *you* inside it, making it work.

*Space Race*

# CHAPTER 1

# The Bullying

The Gwynns had lived just outside the city of York for the past fourteen years. Nesta, their only child, was born there. As far as the neighbors knew, Matthew and Alison Gwynn were a pleasant, young American couple who had settled and made their home in England. Only the faintest of accents and the odd phrase here and there made people remember that they were not British born and bred. They kept themselves to themselves, but so did everyone else in their leafy, comfortable suburb.

Never in a million years would anyone have guessed their astonishing secret.

In fact, the only difficulty they had experienced so far in their time here had been the bullying their daughter had suffered in her first years at Carrick Comprehensive. But that could have happened to any ordinary child, born of purely human parents.

For a year and half, Nesta had been bullied and tormented at school. It was never clear why. She was shy and clever, never one of the crowd, but not friendless. Then one day another girl from the form above, with a long ginger ponytail and eyes like a cat, came up to Nesta in the playground and said, "Is your name *really* Nesta?"

"Yes," said Nesta, not quite sure what this strange girl meant. She did not know her at all.

The girl gave a feline smile, eyes closing almost to slits.

"Where'd you get a name like that from?" she said.

"My mom called me that. She chose it," said Nesta. "It's Welsh for Agnes, I think."

"Mom!" said the girl, with a snigger in her voice. "Who's this *Mom*? Haven't you got a mam then, like the rest of us?"

"I've always called her Mom. It's what she called herself, I suppose. My parents came from Boston two years before I was born. That's in America."

"Oh dear and la-di-dah!" said the girl, tweaking a lock of Nesta's fine hair. Looking at the two of them, the ginger girl would definitely have been the one to stand out in the crowd. Nesta was pale but pretty with gray-blue eyes and soft, light brown hair. She was quite tall for her age but slightly built. The other girl, besides her very distinctive red hair, was large-boned and clumsy-looking. Her complexion was ruddy and she had a wide, toothy grin.

Nesta made no reply and no protest. She felt nonplussed at such uncalled-for attention. She just walked away as quickly as she could.

From such a small beginning, the bullying grew, pushing and shoving, mocking and calling names. The girl, who was known to everyone as Ginger, got a group round her for the wonderful break-time game of tormenting the first-former who never fought back.

Nesta tried hard to stay out of their way, but she told no one, not even her parents. She had felt so ashamed of being singled out. She wept into her pillow at night and wondered, *Why me?*

She couldn't understand what was so special about her. It couldn't just be the name. There were plenty of strange names in the school—a girl called Ethena in 1B, a spotty little boy called Godwin in her own class. No one picked on them.

Her staunch friend in all her troubles was Amy Brown, a short, stocky girl, but very brave despite her lack of height. In the playground, Amy tried to defend Nesta from the bullies. But one against many, no matter how brave, is not always effectual.

"Leave her alone, you lot," Amy said. "She's not doing *you* any harm."

"Who's gonna make us? You?" said Ginger, putting her tongue out at Amy. "You're a shrimp! If you're not careful, we'll add you to the hit list, Goggles!"

"Don't speak to them, Amy," said Nesta anxiously. "It will only make things worse."

Amy tossed her head at the bullies and said, "Touch me and I'll yell so loud I'll be heard from here to the minster."

She might be short and bespectacled, but she bristled in a way that made sure no bully ever ventured too far with her. Nesta, however, was a different proposition altogether. . . .

Even after the summer holidays, the bullying continued. Her second year in the school looked like being no better than the first. The very first day back, Ginger pulled her hair just in passing and said, "See you later, Skinny-pins. Let you know how much we've missed you!"

Nesta looked down at her legs, which were really not especially skinny at all, and wished she were fatter. Would that have made a difference?

"Are my legs really skinny?" she asked Amy.

"They're thinner than mine," said Amy, looking down at her own sturdy legs, "but that doesn't mean anything. I always think my legs are too fat. My brother says I have hockey-player's knees. I'm quite used to insults. It's best to ignore them."

The day that Ginger's friend Lesley punched Nesta in the face and made her nose bleed was the day the bullying reached its peak.

"Do you never fight back, Spike?" said Lesley, a heavy-jowled girl of less than average intelligence. She had caught Nesta in a corner between the wall and the school gate. It was too good a chance to miss.

"No," said Nesta, fearful but firm. "I never fight at all. Fighting is stupid."

Then, quite suddenly, Lesley lifted her fist and leveled it at Nesta's nose. It was a harder blow than she meant to deliver and even she was startled when there was a spurt of blood.

Nesta could hardly believe it had happened. She hurried to the cloakroom to bathe the blood away.

Amy followed her.

"I'm going to tell," she said firmly. She stood with one hand on the washbasin, gripping the rim tightly. "That Ginger and her mates can't get away with this. I won't let them."

Nesta stopped with the paper towel in midair and gave her friend a look of horror. The thought of everyone knowing—teachers, parents, and even any other children who were not yet aware of the situation—was unbearable.

"You can't tell," said Nesta. "Please don't tell. They'll

stop sometime. They'll have to. I never do anything to *them*."

"I'm telling," said Amy grimly, "and nothing you can say will stop me."

She ran out of the cloakroom, up the stairs, and straight to the staffroom door, where she knocked loudly. Mr. Winters opened it.

"Yes?" he said, looking down at Amy over his mug of coffee.

"Please, sir, Ginger Watkins and her gang are bullying Nesta Gwynn. And it's got to stop," said Amy, her chin jutting out determinedly. Harold Winters smiled down at her in amusement, but he took notice all the same. It was the first the staff had known of the problem. The information was acted upon immediately.

Mrs. Powell, the head teacher, rang Mrs. Gwynn. Fortunately, Alison was at home. Arrangements were made for Matthew and Alison to come to the school and discuss the problem. It was agreed between them that Nesta should know nothing about their visit. It is important not to punish the victim.

# CHAPTER 2

# A Lesson for Ginger

Alison Gwynn had long suspected that something was wrong, but Nesta would never admit to it. She would come in from school looking so bleak, and when she smiled at her mother it was as if she were deliberately switching on a happy face.

"How's it going at your new school, honey? You don't seem to have much to say about it." Alison tried not to sound anxious, but it was difficult.

"It's all right," Nesta would say. Then she would busily show her mother the book she had brought home and the tasks she had for homework.

"Have you made any new friends yet? Tell me about them," Alison asked a few weeks into the new term. "I'd like to hear a lot more about your school and what you do there—and I don't just mean French and history!"

"I do have a friend," said Nesta. "She's called Amy Brown."

"Bring her home to tea someday, why don't you?"

"Someday," said Nesta, but she never did. It was too much of a risk. Amy might have told her parents about the bullying, and that would never do.

So the summons to the school, for that was what it felt like, came as no surprise. Matthew took time off work to be there. They sat in Mrs. Powell's room feeling as if somehow they had failed. The head teacher realized how they felt and made every effort to be reassuring.

"We never know the causes of bullying," she said. "I only wish we did. This school is no worse than others. It happens everywhere. Outsiders give all sorts of reasons, but to be honest with you, there is no answer that covers every situation. What we can do in this case is make sure that Nesta is well protected, and that these particular bullies are brought to book."

"How?" said Alison. "What will you do?"

"A fair enough question, Mrs. Gwynn," said Mrs. Powell. "I propose to exclude two of the girls— Amanda Watkins and Lesley Blake—for a fortnight. Their parents will be called in for detailed discussions to make them fully aware of how seriously we view their daughters' behavior. And all of the staff will be told to keep a lookout for any fresh occurrence of bullying. You can be sure that we shall be extra watchful."

"Can I make a different suggestion?"

"Yes?"

"Do nothing," said Alison. "Nothing at all. Just let me have a quiet, civilized word with the ringleader. Here and now, in your presence of course."

"If you think it would do any good," said the head teacher doubtfully.

"I believe it would," said Alison.

When Ginger Watkins came to the head's room, she walked in with a look of defiance on her face. Alison quickly recognized that it was mainly bravado.

"This is Amanda Watkins," said the head teacher, giving the girl a withering look. "Sit down, Amanda. Mrs. Gwynn would like a word with you."

Amanda sat on the edge of the chair Mrs. Powell indicated, a red plastic classroom chair set to one side of the desk so that all three adults could focus their attention upon her. She did not look directly at any of them but held her head high and gazed at the print that hung on the wall above the visitors' heads.

"I am Nesta Gwynn's mother," said Alison, coming straight to the point. "They tell me you are making my daughter's life a misery, Amanda. Is it such good fun to pick on somebody smaller and younger than yourself?"

Ginger glanced at her briefly but did not answer.

"You are, of course, expecting some punishment for your behavior."

Ginger looked warily toward Mrs. Powell. There was

9

something not quite right about this interview. If she'd dared, she would've complained. The glance wavered. Then a voice, a strange, strange voice demanded her attention.

*"Look at me,"* said Alison in words that carried an alien resonance. *"Just look at me."*

Ginger was drawn to look deep into the stranger's dark eyes. Then the oddest thing happened. The room swayed and swirled and everything in it disappeared from her vision. Suddenly she could hear her heart beating. And all she could see was a pair of dark, dark eyes that held her gaze.

There was silence.

The headmistress held her breath. Matthew Gwynn smiled down, a little doubtfully, at the carpet. He knew exactly what his wife was doing and what power she was using. It was impressive.

*"I have asked your head teacher not to punish you,"* said Alison in hollow tones that seemed not to belong to her. *"But I am telling you very firmly that neither you nor any of your friends will ever torment Nesta again."*

She paused till the girl nodded.

*"In fact, Amanda, you will never again bully any child in this school. Do you understand?"*

Ginger felt her mouth go dry so that she had to swallow before she could speak. Whatever illusion Alison was creating, it made the girl feel the complete stupidity of bullying.

"Yes," said Ginger in a voice that cracked as she spoke, "I understand." She blushed to the roots of her hair. Never in her young life had she been so embarrassed. It was a terrible, frozen moment that felt like eternity.

Then Alison spoke briskly in her normal voice.

"With Mrs. Powell's permission," she said, "you may now return to your class."

At that, the room resumed its normal appearance. The walls and the windows, the door, the picture and the furniture were all back in their proper places.

The headmistress nodded vaguely. Ginger stood up and went straight to the door, glad to escape.

"I think you will have no further trouble with Amanda," said Alison after the girl had left. "There will be no need for punishment, and no need to keep any special watch on my daughter."

Then she smiled at the older woman, who still looked puzzled. Josephine Powell was not quite sure, but she fancied she had witnessed some form of mesmerism. It crossed her mind to wonder whether it was legal or moral, but then she rejected such a quibble. Did it work? That was what really mattered!

"I am not sure you should have done that," said Matthew as they made their way home. "We really aren't supposed to use our powers here. We never have done, not in fourteen years; it could be dangerous."

"I don't think so," said Alison. "We have the right to protect ourselves, don't we? And it was a very minor infringement. I didn't attempt to change that girl's personality. I simply brought out what was best in it. Her behavior will change because she knows herself better."

"Maybe," said Matthew. "But Mrs. Powell was puzzled. You could see she was. We must never put ourselves at risk of being discovered."

"There is no risk," said Alison. "The voice perception fades almost immediately; you know it does. The worst that can happen is that Mrs. Powell will think I used some form of hypnosis. But anyone can see that she's a practical person. When she has no further trouble with Amanda, she will be content to let it go. She's too busy a woman to try to mend what's not broken."

A week later, Nesta made a positive move that showed her mother that her somewhat improper intervention had produced the required effect. The problem of bullying had gone away. It was no longer necessary to separate school and home so completely.

"Can I bring Amy home for tea someday, Mom?"

"Of course you can bring Amy home for tea! Any day you want, sweetheart. You know that."

Alison Gwynn had been so pleased to see her daughter looking happy again. Nesta talked quite freely about school and its day-to-day happenings. The autumn term ended and she was actually looking forward to going back to school in the new year.

Then, suddenly, in the middle of January, all of that contentment was threatened. Things began to happen over which neither Nesta nor her parents had any control at all.

The new turn of events was all down to something that occurred in Casselton, nearly a hundred miles away. At Christmas, in that northern town, two people, a father and a son, seemed to have vanished from the face of the earth.

# Starlight, Perhaps

**MINISTER QUESTIONED ABOUT HOSPITAL SECURITY**
*—The Times*

**BOY DISAPPEARS FROM CHILDREN'S WARD**
*—The Guardian*

**ARE OUR CHILDREN SAFE ANYWHERE?** *—The Mirror*

**THE TALE OF A COAT—***The Independent*

**STARLIGHT, PERHAPS—***The Casselton Courier*

The papers carried the story of the disappearance of Patrick Derwent and his son, Thomas, every day for a fortnight. The father had been the first to vanish, after an accident in which a tanker crashed into a post office van. His son had later been somehow spirited away from the hospital where he was being observed because he seemed unable to speak or to identify himself. The facts, however, proved so hard to come by that there came a point where the police were forced to "scale down inquiries." Here was a case that might not be a case at all and was proving totally insoluble. . . .

On Tuesday, the twelfth of January, the postman arrived just as Matthew was getting ready to go out. He rang the doorbell and Matthew hurried to answer him. Alison was upstairs.

"Parcel," said the postman.

"To sign for?" said Matthew.

"No," said the postman. "It was just too big to go through the letterbox."

He handed it over. It was a large floppy package wrapped in soft brown paper.

"Thanks," said Matthew, taking it with both hands and wondering what it could be. A sender address would have helped, but there was none.

Matthew tore open the wrapping on the kitchen table and out fell a whole bundle of newspapers. There was no note to say who had sent them or why. Matthew spread them out on the table and leafed through them one by one. There was a fair assortment of national papers; there were even two editions of a little local paper from Casselton, one that would not normally be seen as far south as York. Whoever had sent them had not troubled to cut out or even mark any relevant stories, just crammed the whole lot into the package so that at first it looked meaningless.

Matthew went back over the bundle and read the headline story. It seemed the obvious thing to do. And it was the right thing! The story that had attracted so many journalists was not just mysterious; for Matthew it was very, very important.

"I just don't know what will come of this," he said to his wife when she came downstairs. He gestured to the pile of newspapers. "It's a good job they came after Nesta went to school."

Their daughter knew nothing about the terrible problem Matthew was about to discuss. She knew very little about her own background at all. Her parents were meant to tell her later, when she had reached maturity. Then would be the time. That was what had been agreed.

Like everyone else in the country, Alison had seen on TV the reports of the disappearance of the man and his son—it had been quite a prominent news item for a day or two, but she had not connected it with herself at all. It was just another odd story. It was only when Matthew showed her the newspaper articles that she realized the full implication.

"Why so many newspapers?" she had asked at first when she saw them strewn over the kitchen table.

"They carry different versions of a story that is of

concern to us. Or maybe it would be better to say that they tell the story from different angles. They don't actually contradict one another as regards the facts. You'll see," said Matthew. "Read this one first."

He passed her the previous Thursday's *Courier*. This was the local Casselton paper, but its headline was the most intriguing. The article beneath it filled a whole page. For this, and for other reasons, it seemed to Matthew to be more dangerous than the others. "Starlight, Perhaps" was all about the two people who had disappeared in Casselton.

It was a long article, much longer than any of the reports in the national press. It bore the byline Shaun Trevelyan. His London editor, who favored the succinct and factual, had dumped Shaun's article. A friend on *The Courier* had been more obliging. It was, after all, a good piece of local news.

Shaun had interviewed practically everyone involved in the affair: the tanker driver and his mate who had been in the road accident that had started it all; nurses and doctors in the hospital where the boy, whose name was given as Thomas Derwent, had been placed when he was in a state of shock after seeing the crash; the villagers in Belthorp where Thomas and his father, Patrick, had lived. And, finally, he had approached their friend and neighbor Stella Dalrymple. She it was who, when asked if she could throw any light on the mystery, had replied with the words that gave the reporter his headline: "Starlight, perhaps . . ." She had closed the door on the young reporter, telling him nothing more. But those two words were quite enough. Shaun Trevelyan had an ear for the music. He was ready to believe that this really was the tale of an alien presence on the planet Earth.

Thomas Derwent had appeared on the local TV channel before his disappearance, a little boy lost whose father was missing. In that interview, the boy had screeched some strange, sound-distorting words at the microphone. These were never repeated on national television because they were not transmittable. Gerry Potterton, the local television reporter, had given Shaun a tape of the "foreign" words the boy had screamed at him, in a voice so strange that the sound system had collapsed under the strain of it. *"Vateelin Tonitheen Ormingat."* That was all the boy had said, just those three words, over and over again, growing louder each time he said them. To decide on their orthography had taken over an hour of listening to the flawed recording. There was no way of conveying the tone and the accent: *Vateelin, Tonitheen,* and *Ormingat* were the best they could manage.

"There's worse," said Matthew, putting aside the earlier papers and turning to the copy of the previous day's *The Courier*. "Read this letter."

He put the paper into Alison's hands.

*Dear Sir,*

*With reference to the story about the boy who went missing from Casselton General Hospital in the middle of the night—I met him. He was in the next bed to me. He spoke to me in his own language. It was hard to understand. But I think the words in the article mean who he is and where he comes from. He told me his name was Tonitheen and that he came from Ormingat. His voice was very, very strange, but he used some English words. I was the only one there who could hear him properly. I have very good hearing. He said "I am" but it sounded odd. And he said "and I come from." So what he really said was "I am Tonitheen and I come from Ormingat." I thought he said "Organmat" but could be wrong. He never mentioned Vateelin to me.*

*I believe he is an alien and that he comes from another planet in outer space. I offered to help him. If he reads this, I want him to know that I will help him anytime he needs me. I liked him. But he might have gone home to his own planet now. Maybe Vateelin is his father and took him away.*

*Yours truly,*
*James Martin (age 10)*
*Hedley Crescent, Casselton*

Alison gasped as she read it.

"How could he get so close to the truth? And what was that child Tonitheen doing telling everyone his name? It is obvious that he and his father are, like us, visitors to Earth. But we are meant never to be known or recognized. They must surely have known that!"

All it needed now was for the UFO enthusiasts to get on the trail!

"There'll be trouble," said Alison after she had finished reading. It was clear that even if the police were no longer actively interested, it was not a matter that would be totally forgotten. The boy's father had disappeared into thin air at the moment when the tanker driver and his mate were sure that they had run him over. All that he left behind was a strip of sheepskin torn from his overcoat. And it was this coat that had been found on the hospital bed after the boy vanished.

"Nothing like this has ever happened before," said Matthew, looking anxiously from one paper to the next. "I don't know what sort of danger it puts us in, but there will be repercussions, that's for sure—especially for us. Casselton is less than a hundred miles away. Our people are clearly concerned. Why else would we have been sent these papers?"

Alison raised her eyebrows, as much as to say, How do you know who sent them?

"Who else would be sending us newspapers like this?" said Matthew. He had already looked at the postmark on the package but it was too blurred to read.

Matthew's next home contact was not due till the

first of June. For fourteen years, he had followed the strictly laid down routine. His annual holiday was always arranged around it. Now he felt sure that there would be some earlier communication.

He looked up at the kitchen clock.

"I'll have to go to work now," he said, "but I'll arrange to have the rest of the week as holiday. This is an emergency."

Alison went with him to the front door.

"What about Nesta?" she said. "Will she need to know?"

"I think so," he said, looking at his wife quite vaguely, as if he weren't quite sure of anything yet. "I don't see any other way. There'll be a follow-up to those newspapers. You must see that."

"I don't know," said Alison. "It might all blow over. We could leave it a week or two."

"Common sense tells me that it won't," said her husband. "Those newspapers tell us that it won't. Besides, it is only bringing forward what would have happened in any case, six years from now."

"You think we'll be recalled?" said his wife, startled at the thought of the upheaval. She was loyal to Ormingat. There was no question about that, but Earth had been her home for so long now. And it wasn't such a bad place after all, especially not England, and, most especially, not York.

"I feel sure we will," said Matthew. "All this publicity

21

makes our recall inevitable. You know how careful they are. They will not jeopardize two hundred and fifty years of quiet research."

He put one arm around her shoulders.

"And look at it this way," he added. "We do love our real home. Our time here has often felt like exile. And as for Nesta, you did as you were told. Somewhere in the back of her mind is the story of the Faraway Planet. She will easily relate it to the truth you tell her now. She is a very intelligent girl."

As the door closed behind her husband, Alison thought how simple life would be if everything were as black and white as Matthew managed to paint it. The psychologists of Ormingat might be right: it might work as they had said it would. But there was the possibility that they could be wrong.

*My poor Nesta*, she thought, *this is the wrong time and the wrong way for you to learn the truth!*

The story of the Faraway Planet that Nesta had been told in her baby years had been deliberately made to sound like a fairy tale. Even the real name of the planet had been left unspoken.

How well Nesta's mother remembered telling her daughter that bedtime story!

# CHAPTER 4

# The Faraway Planet

"Tell me about the Faraway Planet where you used to live before I was born," Nesta would say, all those years ago, when her mother came to tuck her up in bed. It was one of her favorite bedtime stories. Alison had been instructed to plant it there, alongside "The Goose Girl," "Rapunzel," and "Little Tom Thumb."

"Long, long ago," she would begin, "Daddy and I lived with our friends and our families in a sort of castle—or that is what *this* world would probably call it. The outer walls of the castle rose up in curves and spirals to a sky that by day was pale blue and sometimes golden, but never too bright and never too dull, never gray and never cloudy. No stones formed these walls, nothing so hard. And there were no sharp corners anywhere for you to bump yourself on."

"A bouncy castle," Nesta said once, after they had been to the fete on the playing field.

Alison laughed and said, "Bigger by far, and not at all bouncy. Just think how uncomfortable that would be!"

"And the walls inside," Nesta prompted, ready for the next bit of the story.

"The walls inside the castle had a pearly glow that gave light by night or by day, even after our twin suns had set. Just as well, for a night and day were more topsy-turvy there than here. Our planet took a course like a figure eight, turning first round one sun, then the next. And it still does, you know, even though we are not there to see it."

"Draw it," said Nesta. And when her mother had drawn the planet's orbit in crayon on a large sheet of sugar paper, one loop much larger than the other, Nesta would trace her finger round and round it, enjoying the neverendingness. It was a shape that she would always find pleasing, even after she had forgotten why. The wax of the crayon and the roughness of the paper sustained the memory.

"Now tell me what the planet is called," Nesta would demand after the figure-of-eight game palled. Alison's dark eyes would glisten when this demand was made. The name of the planet was on the tip of her tongue and she longed to say it. But that was strictly against the rules.

"I can't," she said, holding both of Nesta's hands in hers, "not yet. It is a very secret name and you, my darling, are much too little to be told. When you are very big and very wise, then I will be able to whisper the name in your ear, and you will be as thrilled to hear it as I shall be to tell."

"Tell me about the doors," said Nesta, accepting the answer that her mother always gave. She drew her knees up to her chin expectantly. The doors were a very good part of the story, much easier to follow and understand.

Nesta would look at her mother's dark, curly hair and smiling face and wait for all the actions that went with this description. Alison would spread her hands in a sort of swirl, as if she were a magician. Past became present as she invoked this castle in the air.

"The doors are like no doors you have ever seen. They are set in huge, curved arches, and when we leave or enter they roll aside like magic mist, and in them are all the colors of the rainbow—and a few more shades that do not even exist here on Earth. They have no purpose other than to shut out the breeze and to mark the outside from the in. There are no bad people anywhere on the planet; so there is no need to lock anyone out. No one there would ever hurt anyone else. Every single thing is share and share alike, though of these things they share, I cannot tell you. There are no Earth words to describe them, and there is nothing on Earth to which they bear any real likeness."

"Say something *not* an Earth word," said Nesta, snuggling down into her bed again. She knew what the answer would be, but she always asked because that was part of the ritual. And there was always the faint possibility that someday the answer might be different.

"Not yet," said her mother with a laugh. "The language of the Other Place does not belong here. It would sound too strange: the atmosphere on Earth is all wrong for it."

Nesta let that go—it was what she had been told many times before in many different ways. She had a child's wise way with things she did not understand. She simply skipped over them.

"And the people there? What do they look like?" she said eagerly, waiting for the smallest addition to words she had already heard.

Alison looked down at her little daughter, the light brown hair spread on her pillow, the gray-blue eyes returning her gaze earnestly.

"Beautiful," she said. "In their own special way, they are more beautiful than the fairest of mankind. At home—for it is our home—we have our own bodies. These that we have here are just garments we must wear for our time on Earth. They are pretty nice garments, but not as good as the real thing!"

"Me too?" said the child, already aware that there was a flaw in this story somewhere. She had been born here in the city of York. She had never known anywhere else. She knew that she more closely resembled her father but that people said she had her mother's smile. Sometimes she wished her hair were thick and curly like Mom's. Sometimes she wondered how a smile could be separated from the rest of the face!

"Can I take off my fingers?" Nesta asked one night, finding a new question for the old story when her mother came again to the part about their Earth bodies being garments. Her left hand tugged tentatively at the fingers on her right. After all, *clothes* were things to wear and *they* could be removed. People wear nothing at all in the bath!

Alison smiled. But secretly she felt sad. Once Nesta began asking difficult questions, the storytelling would have to stop. It must not continue into the age of reason. To let a child know too much is to risk betrayal.

"It doesn't work like that," said Alison carefully. "It is much more complicated. Someday you will know all about it. Then you will understand."

"But *I* wasn't born in that place you came from," Nesta said.

"No," said her mother. "When we left home, we had no idea what a wonder we had in store for us. You were a sort of bonus, a lovely, smiley, cuddly bonus. You didn't 'go with the job'! Daddy and I still marvel that you are ours."

Nesta caught the word *job* and said, "Daddy works in the bank. That is his job."

27

"Yes," said Alison, content to leave it at that. "Daddy works at the bank."

"Now tell about how you got here," said Nesta. "Tell about the spaceship."

"Our spaceship was no bigger than a baseball. It was a crystalline and shimmering blue, yet changing constantly as if it were a living thing. To go inside it we diminished—you know that word by now. We became so small that the inside of the ship seemed to us bigger than a house. That is where we lived for three years, traveling through space, learning things, and preparing for our stay here on Earth."

The story was sometimes embroidered with other snippets. Like the time Alison went on to say, "And we arrived in the exact spot prepared for us. That was a rare and wonderful thing! To come so far and to arrive spot-on, in the right place, is not easy. We were warned about that. The spaceship could have veered off course and landed miles away. Then we would have had to set out and find this house in this fair city, where it was all ready and waiting for us!"

"Who got it ready?" said Nesta.

"Others from the Faraway Planet, secret workers. We never see them—but we know that they are there, like the elves who help the shoemaker!"

"Where is the spaceship now?" said Nesta. "When are you going to tell me where it is?"

"Not yet," said her mother. "Someday, when you are

older. For now, I can only say that it is safe, buried deep in the earth but ready to leave when the time comes, ready to take us all home."

That was where the story always ended. And the game finished.

Nesta yawned, lids drooping over the gray-blue eyes. Before entering the Land of Nod, she said sleepily, wanting to be reassured that this was just a story after all, "But we're really Americans, aren't we? And you and Daddy came from Boston."

"Americans of Welsh descent," said Alison softly. "The Gwynns are a very old family and that, for now at least, is who we are."

So the story of the Faraway Planet could safely take its place alongside "The Little Matchgirl," "The Tin Soldier," and "Cinderella." There were so many different stories, but none of them was really, really true. Young as she was, she already knew that. Children are born knowing that stories are safe.

Nesta's eyes shut tight. She was fast asleep.

Alison bent over and kissed her, stroking the soft hair back from her forehead.

*"Nallytan, Neshayla ban,"* she said very softly in tones not of this earth, and in a language that was definitely not English, and not even Welsh.

# CHAPTER 5

# The Signal

On the Wednesday of that week in January, Matthew stayed home, tensely waiting. Nesta went off to school as usual, unaware that anything untoward was happening. She was always the first to leave the house: school was a good long bus ride away. Matthew's bank was much closer and he usually went by car. Alison's work at the university was part-time, and much of it she did at home.

"I think you should tell her tonight," said Matthew. "We can both tell her, if you like, but I think she will be more comfortable hearing it from you."

Alison gave her husband a look of amusement. She had long since grown to know and love his Earth face—his crinkled fair hair that never looked quite as neat as it should, his blue eyes that were wide and innocent. On their home planet, he had looked very different, of course, but the character that looked out of those innocent eyes was the same. He was the dreamer of dreams; she was the practical one.

"I think we should wait till you know that they want to talk to you," she said. "There has been no signal yet. If you have to go for instructions, then I shall be left alone with Nesta, for however long it takes. Then will be time enough to tell her."

Matthew still looked worried.

"We don't even know what the signal will be. This has never arisen before. What if I don't recognize it?"

"You will," said Alison. "There would be no point otherwise. And if no signal comes within the next three days, I think you should enter the ship in any case."

"I can't do that!" said Matthew. "How could I do that? Unless I am wanted, it won't let me in."

"And if it won't let you in," said his wife logically, "then you mustn't be wanted and we can just forget all about it till June."

But the signal did come. And in a way that was surprisingly easy.

Early on Thursday morning, well before daylight, the clock radio by their bed began to buzz like an angry bee. The buzz grew louder till first Alison and then Matthew woke up. Alison stared in silence at the clock's red digits, but her tired senses could not register the time.

"What on earth is that?" said Matthew, yawning.

At the sound of his voice, the buzzing stopped.

Then a voice he recognized—a metallic, staccato voice—began to speak. Matthew had heard it every year for the past fourteen years; every year from the first to the third of June, this voice had fed him information and asked him questions. Now it was speaking out of the radio in his room. Its English, as always, was not quite on key and sounded foreign. Its timbre was much more metallic than usual, as if this unaccustomed medium interfered with its clarity.

"You-have-heard-the-news," it grated. "There-is-need-to-instruct. Tomorrow-after-sunset-you-must-come-to-the-source."

That was all. The clock went back to being its normal self.

"So that's it," said Matthew. He sat up and swung his feet to the floor.

"That's it," said Alison with a sigh. "But do get back into bed, Mattie. It's only four o'clock. It will be easier to think it all out in the morning. These Earth bodies need their sleep!"

On Friday Nesta set off for school totally unaware of the shocks life had in store for her. Alison went with her to the gate, not something she always did, but not altogether unusual.

"Take care," Alison said, giving Nesta a parting hug.

"I will, Mom," said Nesta, smiling. "Take care, yourself!"

"It looks like rain," said her mother. "Have you got your umbrella?"

"Here in my bag," said Nesta, pointing down to the pouch that held it.

"Well, bye then, and take care," said Alison again.

Nesta gave her a quizzical look.

"Have you got a premonition or something?" she said with a laugh. "I always take care! And if I don't go soon, I'll miss the bus!"

Alison stood and watched her to the end of the street, where she turned and waved.

"Did you say anything to her?" asked Matthew when she went indoors.

"No, not yet. This afternoon will be time enough. What could I possibly say in five minutes?"

They sat by the fire, saying little but thinking more.

"I *do* want to go back," said Matthew after one long silence. "The will-o'-the-wisp memory of Ormingat haunts me, as if there were a great emptiness in my life. There are mornings even now when I feel like poor old Caliban, awakening from a dream of sounds that give delight and hurt not. . . ."

"I know," said Alison, not totally convinced. "And the joy of going home ought to be uppermost in my mind too, but this is home for me now, this Earth, this town, this street, this house. Oh, Mattie, I love England as if I had been born here."

"You will carry the memory with you, *Athelerane*," said Matthew softly. "It will be part of your being."

"Like the memory of Ormingat?" said his wife with a smile enigmatic and sad.

"Probably," said Matthew, taking her hand in his. "It is not such a bad way to remember."

But his imagination went far beyond hers. His vision of Ormingat was spiritual; hers was physical and somehow false. No two things in the universe are totally identical; and those who think have each their own array of thoughts.

At three o'clock, Matthew and Alison went out in silence to drain the pond at the bottom of the back garden. It was not raining, but moisture hung in the air and Matthew's hand and arm were chilled to the bone as he reached down into the pondweed to pull out the plug.

"Now we shall wait for Nesta," said Alison as the water drained sluggishly away, leaving slimy green fronds clinging to the basin. It was not quite like the normal garden pond. In its center, on a great stone lily pad, sat what can be best described as a monolith, carved in the form of a frog.

# CHAPTER 6

# The Shock

When Nesta came home from school, it was already dusk. She let herself into the house, as she always did, and called out, "Mom, I'm home."

The answer came from the direction of the kitchen.

"Your father and I are in the back garden, Nesta," said her mother's voice. "There's something we have to show you. Come straight out."

Nesta hurried through the kitchen to the back of the house, wondering what the something could be. The light above the porch was lit, but the garden itself was in shade. Nesta was puzzled as to what they should have to show her out there on such a dull, cold afternoon.

Her mother was wearing her thick fleece jacket and

winter boots. She was standing, arms folded, outside on the patio. Her smile, as she looked at her daughter, was a little nervous. This way of doing things had been her husband's idea; Alison was not at all sure that it was really the best way. But she had not been able to think of a better, given how little time there was.

"We've drained the pond," she said, "but we waited for you to come home before moving the frog from its pad."

Nesta was mystified.

"But it's not June," she said, looking from one parent to the other. "We only ever move the frog on the first of June."

"The day your father goes on his business trip," said her mother very deliberately. "But the trip is earlier this year."

Every year, on the first of June, Matthew would go away for three days on a "business trip." This was what her parents called it, and Nesta did not bother to question them. It was clearly something to do with his work at the bank. So Nesta thought.

There was just this one strange ritual that might have made it seem different. The night before he left, the pond in the back garden was always drained and the gray stone frog that squatted in the center was lifted, with difficulty, from its gray stone lily pad. It was possibly the biggest, heaviest garden ornament in the world, created by some weird, outlandish sculptor obsessed with incongruous size, a bulldozer of a bullfrog if ever there was one!

For as long as she could remember, Nesta had watched the fun as her parents lugged the monster onto the lawn. When Father came home, the whole thing would go into reverse: the frog would sit once more on its pad and the pond would be refilled with water. The pond itself was quite modest, a shallow moat around the statue.

Nesta gave her mother a look of astonishment. Till now it had seemed that draining the pond was a thing to do in early summer, maybe to clean it. That it had always coincided with her father's departure had been just that—pure coincidence. They could not possibly be connected.

Could they?

"But—but . . . what has draining the pond to do with it? And moving the frog?"

"You'll see," said her mother. "You will be amazed, shocked even, but we can't think of any other way to make you believe the thing we have to tell you."

Matthew stood by, looking uncomfortable. Even he was not completely sure how his idea would work out.

"We should move the frog now," he said. "There's no point in waiting any longer. It'll soon be pitch-dark."

So he and Alison stepped down into the basin of the pond and stood on either side of the large stone frog. They gripped it with both hands.

"Push," said Matthew.

"Pull," said Alison. "Pull harder."

The soles of her boots slid against the wet pond-weed. Gripping the cold stone was numbing her fingers. It was definitely harder to move in winter than in summer. For some minutes it seemed as if it would not move at all.

Then, at long last, the frog gave a groan and swung over from the pad, up the pond basin, and onto the lawn, Matthew and Alison rolling it to its usual resting place.

"Phew!" said Alison. "That thing must weigh a ton! It never gets any easier!"

"Now I suppose we go into the house," said Nesta, eyeing both parents apprehensively, "and Father gets ready to go."

At that moment the only explanation she could come up with for their strange behavior was that this must be some New England superstition. Take a St. Christopher medal in the car. . . . Drain the garden pond and move the frog before you go on a journey. . . .

Surely her parents were too intelligent to think like that?

But it got worse.

"Not this time," said her mother. "This time we miss out the charade. Your father is ready to go now, and *that* is where he is going."

She pointed to the center of the lily pad.

"Do you remember the story of the Faraway Planet?" she said softly. "The one I told you when you were very young?"

Nesta *did* remember. She had not thought of it for years. But she did remember. Thinking back, it was not quite like the other fairy tales: it had a place and some activity, but no beginning or end. The characters were not elves or fairies but her own mother and father. The main event was just a journey, safely accomplished in an incredibly small spaceship.

"That story," said her mother carefully, "is true. The secret name of the planet, I can tell now, is Ormingat. Tonight you are going to see evidence of the truth of the story, not the whole truth, but enough to show you that it is more than just another fairy tale."

Nesta looked appalled. It seemed to her now that one or both of her parents had gone completely insane. Matthew realized how bewildered she was, and how much more bewildered she was about to be. He put his arms around her and gave her a hug.

"Don't worry," he said, "it will be all right. It will be more all right than you can possibly imagine."

Alison gave her husband a look of impatience. It was no use being so hopeful at this stage. Nesta was already rejecting what they were trying to tell her. That was only too clear.

"Come by me," said her mother, "and I shall try to

explain exactly what is going to happen next. In the very center of the lily pad there is a shaft leading down into the earth. That is where our spaceship is, sinking lower down each year. From the very start, our stay was scheduled to be for twenty years. After that, our engineers say that the depth will be too great: the ship is being pulled by gravity. It is very heavy and very dense. Every year, your father goes down and checks everything. He communicates with Ormingat, gives information about Earth and its people, and receives instructions for the year ahead. Other observers work in different ways: we are long-term operatives and that is our way."

Alison paused, giving her daughter a chance to digest this, a chance to speak. The old story had been intended to support this revelation, to make their daughter more ready to accept the truth of it. A vain hope!

Nesta simply looked at her mother in dazed amazement. Her parents were mad; they were both mad. No other explanation would come to mind. It was frightening. She was being asked to believe the impossible.

"To go into the spaceship," continued her mother, "he has to diminish—you remember the word? It was one you always liked. Every part of him becomes smaller till he is small enough to enter a different dimension."

"Ye-es," said Nesta slowly, giving both parents a cautious look. "Then does he fly away for his business trip?"

It was as if she had decided to humor their insanity. These could not be the parents she had known and loved all her life.

"No," said her mother with a laugh, "he is never further than the bottom of the garden. The spaceship will not move till it is ready to return to Ormingat. But watch now: actions speak louder than words. Stand here with me."

It was cold and, though it wasn't raining, the air was damp. Nesta was still wearing her school coat, but she shivered. She really did not know what to think. Even the way her mother spoke the name of the planet was so foreign she could not hear it properly, and the voice could have been that of a ventriloquist. What on earth were they up to?

"I hate jokes," she muttered into her collar, suddenly feeling that if they were not mad they must be up to some stupid trick. Stupid was preferable, but irritating. "I'm too old for silly games."

"Hush," said her mother. "It's not a game. Just wait and see."

Matthew said nothing.

He walked away from them into the gloom. But his outline was still clearly visible as he stepped down into the circle of cement that formed the bowl of the pond. He went to the center, bent down, and reached with his right hand into the middle of the lily pad. There was a sudden shaft of blue light, like a brief flash of lightning. Then Matthew shrank into the earth as if he had liquefied. In the blink of an eye, no part of him was visible.

Nesta gasped. Then she slumped against her mother in a dead faint. It took some seconds for her to become even semiconscious again. Alison held her up and half-carried her into the house.

CHAPTER 7

# Let It Not Be True

For the second time in less than a year, Alison used the power of Ormingat, a weak strain admittedly, but adequate for use on Earth. This time her reason was more urgent. This time she felt not the slightest guilt: the power was passing from like to like, from mother to daughter.

Nesta was lying stiffly on the sofa, still in her outdoor coat. Her eyes were open but glazed, and she was trembling in every limb. She had just seen her father disappear into the earth. An ordinary, solid human being had been sucked into nothingness before her very eyes. This was a shock on a massive scale. The heart might fail with it; the brain might snap.

"Heal hands," said Alison urgently, touching the

slim fingers that quivered uncontrolled. The hands grew still and the body turned limp.

"Heal little heart," said Alison as she gently undid the buttons on Nesta's coat and drew unresisting arms from each sleeve.

"Heal mind and soul and understanding," she said, holding her daughter's head between her hands.

For moments that seemed interminable, nothing happened.

"Mind and soul and understanding, heal!" Alison said quite harshly, willing the power to be strong enough.

Then she gave a sigh of relief as her daughter's eyes lost their trancelike gaze.

Nesta looked directly at her mother and said sharply, "Why did you never tell me about this before? I had a right to know."

Alison sat down beside her daughter on the sofa, one arm round her shoulders. Dusk had turned to dark and the room was lit only by the firelight.

"Children cannot be told things that they might even accidentally betray," she said.

"I am nearly thirteen," said Nesta. "I am not a child."

"No," said her mother, "but you are not far from childhood."

"And all that about the Faraway Planet?" said Nesta, remembering the old story and trying to make sense of it. "You muddled it all up with the elves and the shoemaker. And you let me go on thinking that you came from Boston. You don't come from Boston?"

"No," said her mother. "We have never been anywhere near Boston. When I told you that story you really were a child and I was bound to tell you childish things. The truth was disguised as fiction because that was deemed safer—to plant a hint in your mind, like a seed buried in soil. The real fiction was always Boston, not just for you but also for the world outside. And it had to sound as genuine as possible."

"But you told me you lived on St. Botolph's Street, and that Granny Morgan's house was high up on Beacon Hill," said Nesta, dredging up what she had long believed were facts. "You showed me on the map. You said how you took rides in the swan boats on the pond in the park and played tag on Boston Common when you were very young. Was that all made up?"

"You won't understand this," said Alison, feeling cornered by these questions. "It is almost impossible to explain. But we *do* remember Boston as if we had been there. Sometimes we ourselves find it difficult to distinguish between genuine and implanted memories. For our time on Earth, the implanted memories are stronger. They have to be."

"And you never flew on the Concorde?" said Nesta, nervously rucking up memories as if they were made of cloth.

"We think we did," said her mother, "but we know

we didn't. That is a dichotomy we have learnt to live with."

At a stroke, Nesta was deprived of the whole of her family history. She had long accepted the early deaths of her grandparents, each from different causes and at different times. Her granny Morgan had been the last to die: back there in Boston, of heart disease, when Nesta was just four years old.

After that, so she had been told, her parents had lost all contact with their old home. Neither parent had ever laid claim to brothers or sisters, just friends; and friendship fades. "People change and move off in different directions. They lose touch," her father had said. So the broken ties had been neatly shrugged off; but the history was still comfortably there, giving shape and form to life. Now all of it was blown away and, as far as Nesta could see, there was nothing else to put in its place. The emptiness was unbearable.

A dark thought came uninvited into her heart and soul. If she had no ancestors, no earthly place of origin, where then was God?

"I don't want to know this," she sobbed, clenching her hands so that her nails bit into the palms. "It's a dream. It has to be."

"It's not a dream," said her mother gently, "and it is not bad, not at all bad. The story of the Faraway Planet was mostly true: we did come here in that spaceship and it really is no bigger than a handball. There is nothing bad or sinister about it—it is simply Ormingat science. It is not magic. Our experts know how to do things that the people of Earth cannot begin to comprehend."

"*I* am one of the people of Earth," said Nesta. "I was born here in York. I have never traveled out of England."

"That won't always be so," said her mother. "You were destined from birth to travel far and to come into your own."

Then Alison went on to explain that very soon, much sooner than they had anticipated, it was quite probable that they would all be going to Ormingat. They would enter the spaceship together and travel home. They would become their true selves, body and soul.

The idea of "going home" to this Faraway Planet seemed dreadful to Nesta. The thought of it made her angry. Her parents, who claimed to be such upright tellers of truth, had been living a lie for years and years! She felt betrayed and confused.

"All I have ever wanted was to be like everybody else!" she said. "When I was bullied at school, the thing I minded most was being different. This is worse; this is much, much worse. I don't want to believe you. And I don't want to change into some sort of alien."

Alison held her closer and sighed.

"It's not what you think," she said. "It isn't sudden or

terrible. The journey home will take three years. On that journey, the shape and texture of your body will very, very gradually change, no more than that. I just wanted to let you know that the change will be a good one. Nothing bad is going to happen to you."

Nesta sat upright, shaking off her mother's arm.

"You don't even know if I have an 'Orpingat' body," she said abruptly. "The body—or whatever you call it—I have now is the one I was born with. And you and Father might be able to diminish, but you can't be sure that I can."

"You can," said her mother firmly. "We know you can. When you were six months old I had to take you into the spaceship to be presented and have your name entwined with you."

"Entwined? Nesta?" said her daughter.

"*Neshayla,*" said Alison softly, in the same strange voice she used in naming the Faraway Planet, and, though it was spoken deliberately low, its tone was still unearthly. Even the English words were colored by the proximity of this voice. They bore an accent distinctly foreign. "And I am *Athelerane.*"

"And Father?" said Nesta, fascinated in spite of herself.

"He is *Maffaylie.*"

The voice that vibrated on these names made Nesta shiver.

Alison got up, put on the light, and closed the curtains.

"I think we should have supper now and go to bed," she said in her normal mid-Atlantic accent. "It may be some days before your father returns. It is better if we sleep. We can talk more tomorrow."

Nesta did not sleep. She lay in the darkness and tried to remember every detail of the Faraway Planet story. She prayed for the problem to go away. *Please, God, let me sleep now and wake up tomorrow morning to find that none of this is true.*

# CHAPTER 8

# Explanations

After a night of tossing and turning, feeling so feverish that she flung the covers from her bed, Nesta was longing for morning to come.

The clock by her bed crept from seven to eight. Drifting in and out of reverie, she waited for the dawn. However gray and bleak it might be, it would be welcome. Then she heard her mother moving around in the house. It was Saturday morning, a time of later rising than on weekdays.

With just the faintest hope that her father would be sitting at the breakfast table, that the events of the night before had been no more than a very vivid dream, Nesta got dressed and went downstairs. But in the kitchen, she found only her mother. Alison was sitting waiting for her, waiting nervously and trying hard to appear calm.

"Have your breakfast first," she said. "Then I have things to show you."

To one side of the breakfast table there was a pile of newspapers.

Nesta glanced at them but said nothing. She was still angry and shocked and doubtful. She poured herself a cup of coffee and accepted toast and marmalade. It was as if something fragile was about to be broken, reality ready to be smashed to smithereens. She would not be the first to speak of it.

"That's all I want this morning," she said. "I don't feel hungry."

Alison sat by her, drinking coffee but eating nothing.

"Everything that happened last night is true," said Alison very deliberately. "I know you're hoping it was just a dream. That's understandable. But it *is* true. And there is much more I have to tell you."

Nesta gave her a sharp look but persisted in saying nothing.

"The reason your father had to go into the spaceship yesterday is to do with the stories in these newspapers."

She put one hand on top of the pile of papers, flat as if swearing on the Bible. The resemblance flashed across Nesta's mind and she half-smiled grimly.

"You remember the story of the boy who disappeared from the hospital in Casselton?" Alison said. "It was on TV last week. An overcoat was left on his bed. It is believed to belong to his father, though his father had already vanished in a mysterious way."

"Yes," said Nesta reluctantly. "I know. I watched it, same as everybody else."

Alison handed her one of the newspapers, open at the right place.

"Read that one first," she said.

After Nesta had read everything, including the letter from James Martin, she sat back and said, "So you think that this boy and his father are from outer space, and that the people writing about it are becoming suspicious?"

"Strongly suspicious," said Alison, "and likely to become more so. It will go quiet, and then all sorts of security people will be secretly prying and investigating."

"And what has that to do with us? How do you connect it up?" said Nesta coldly.

"The names," said Alison. "Quite apart from anything else, the names give it away. Until now, no one on Earth has known the name of Ormingat. No one has ever suspected a thing. We have visited for the best part of three Earth centuries, watching carefully and acquiring all sorts of knowledge."

"And that is why you came here?"

"No. In the beginning, we came as explorers. Then we realized what a mixed-up place Earth was. Clever, yes, but so mindlessly aggressive! Our people became concerned in case Earthlings should ever acquire the ability to reach Ormingat. No one knows how we would handle the problem of a hostile alien invasion. Ours is a peaceful planet. So, all those years ago, it was decided that Earth must be one of our areas of study. We were to learn all we could about it."

Alison paused and smiled wistfully. Learning was for her a way of life.

"And it was far from wasteful," she went on, "even without the prospect of invasion. Much of the knowledge turned out to be wonderful and well worth adding to our own culture. Yet, after all these years, there is still the dark side: wars and famine and pestilence. That is something we find so hard to understand."

"Aren't you looking in the wrong place then?" said Nesta with a trace of sarcasm in her voice. "York is not poverty stricken. There's no war or famine here. A local flood is a major event."

"No," said her mother, "I agree with you. We have had the easiest of missions. Our job is cultural research. We are not scientists or anthropologists. But there could be Ormingatrig anywhere on Earth. We are not allowed to know who they are or where they are. We are not here to conquer or to colonize. One

53

way or another, we are here to learn. Others may not be as lucky as we are."

Nesta by now was well on her way to believing the story, but that did not make her like it any better. There had always been something within her that seemed to set her apart. The implanted fairy tale must have done its job after all.

"We're not so lucky now," she said flatly. "If you expect me to leave here and go to a place that to me is unknown and unwanted, I can't count myself as lucky, no matter how beautiful your planet of Ormingat might be. It is yours, not mine."

"Take time to think about it," said her mother. "I know it seems strange, but to be different is not always bad. Think of yourself not so much as different, but as very special."

 Breakfast was over. The newspapers were stashed away in the bottom drawer of the bureau.

"What will you do today?" said Alison, almost as if everything were normal. "I am going into town, if you'd like to come. We can have lunch at Betty's. There's no point in sitting around here just waiting. I don't suppose your father will be home for at least another day, maybe longer."

"I already told you, Mom, I promised to meet Amy," said Nesta, deliberately copying her mother's casual tone. "We're going to look at hockey boots. Amy has been picked for the junior team. It's something new they're trying out."

"That's fine," said her mother, "but remember you must not tell her anything about all this. I can't stress too much how important it is to stay silent."

"What do you take me for?" said Nesta indignantly, her eyes more gray than blue at that moment. "I wouldn't tell her even if I could. She'd think I wasn't all there."

Nesta was becoming increasingly streetwise. School had done that much for her. She used expressions now that she never heard at home. Yet coming from her, they sounded strange, as if she were not meant to talk in that way.

# CHAPTER 9

# Stella's Visitors

The Gwynns were not the only ones to pay special attention to the articles in *The Casselton Courier*.

On the fifth floor of a government building in Manchester is the office of a very small but efficient department that deals entirely in reports of sightings of UFOs or any other strange phenomena that might indicate the presence of extraterrestrial beings anywhere in Britain. Other departments would also pick up this sort of information, but their interests would be more pedestrian, concerned with things like airspace, national defense, and smuggling. Manchester's Extraterrestrial Department was directed entirely at the possibility that there could be intelligent beings from some other galaxy infiltrating our ecosystem.

"This may be of interest," said Mrs. Ames, the office secretary. In her hand she had the article that had come in the morning post. It had been sent from Casselton by one of their amateur observers: an account of the disappearance of Thomas Derwent from Casselton General Hospital.

Rupert Shawcross read the article with more than usual interest. Casselton was his hometown, though his visits there over the past thirty years had been few and far between.

"Might be worth looking into," he said.

"Shall I ask Charles to go? Next week sometime?"

"No," said Rupert, "I'll go myself. Book me in somewhere for, well, let's say, Wednesday, Thursday, and Friday night. That'll give me time to see the local police and follow up any leads."

Mrs. Ames raised her eyebrows. Rupert did not usually volunteer to do the legwork. He was more into collating and working on the computer. Pale-eyed and pale-skinned, he seldom saw the light of day. Whenever possible, he left outside duties to his younger colleagues.

"Not your usual method of inquiry," said Mrs. Ames, slightly mocking, though that was something Rupert would not perceive.

"I know the area," he said dryly. "I was born there. I might see something others could miss."

So it was that on Thursday, the fourteenth of January, Inspector Galway and the man from the ministry were together at Stella Dalrymple's front door in the village of Belthorp.

Stella was expecting them and even knew the purpose of the visit. The meetings the inspector had already had with her had made him very careful to keep her properly informed. Her anger when told of Thomas's disappearance was still only too clear in Inspector Galway's mind! That was before he had shown her the coat, of course. Her reaction to the finding of the coat still seemed odd to him, if only because she did not seem to be quite as mystified as everybody else.

"Come in, Inspector," she said, opening the door wide. "And you must be Mr. Shawcross?"

"Yes," said Rupert uncomfortably. He felt more at home dealing with pieces of paper or, better still, feeding data into a computer. After so many warnings about the lady he was about to interview, he was not sure what to expect. She looked quite normal—attractive really, with that copper-colored hair and slim figure. She was not young, but she was not old either. She was certainly no battle-ax. And really, all Inspector Galway had said was that Mrs. Dalrymple was a very forthright and determined woman.

She sat them in her front room and gave them tea and biscuits.

"Now," she said briskly, "I don't think I can tell you anything about Thomas or Patrick that you don't know already. But you are welcome to ask."

"Well," said the inspector, "I think I had better begin by revising what you do know, for Mr. Shawcross's information."

"Rupert," said Mr. Shawcross, smiling in a friendly way over his cup.

"Rupert," said the inspector, swallowing anxiously. How would Mrs. Dalrymple respond?

"Stella," she said, smiling back at the visitor. Then she turned to the inspector and said, almost mischievously, "So what do we call you?"

"John," he said, relieved. Perhaps it was going to be less difficult than he'd thought. Being less formal might help to make the interview easier. Though any interview with Stella Dalrymple was bound to have its dangerous moments at this time.

"So," he went on, "Rupert already knows that you were friend and neighbor to the Derwents for four or five years."

"Five," said Stella, "and not just a friend and neighbor. I was employed by Patrick to look after Thomas whilst he was at work. I did that for practically the whole of the time that they were here. They became almost family to me."

On the last words, she felt something like a sob

creep into her throat. She had been prepared for this meeting and determined to keep calm. But it was not easy.

John Galway looked at her sharply, concerned that they might be upsetting her. He knew how much she loved the boy; the little he had seen of her had made him very aware of that.

Stella caught his look and said quickly, "I *am* unhappy. But I have agreed to answer your questions, so far as I am able. So don't worry. Life has to go on. People have to cope with whatever happens."

"But what did happen?" said Rupert. "What do you think happened?"

Unlike the inspector, Rupert was very much the man from the ministry, anxious to find out what he needed to know. Even the bonhomie and the first-name terms were artificial; they served a purpose. Given the choice, Rupert would happily have dispensed with the flummery and got straight to the point.

Stella looked at him and knew his true worth. His eyes lacked warmth.

"Patrick disappeared after a crash on Walgate Hill in Casselton," she said. "The drivers of the brewery tanker involved in the crash thought they had run him over. But the only trace of him was a strip torn from his sheepskin coat that they found stuck to one of the wheels."

John Galway appreciated Stella's control and knew

that Rupert's visit would get him nowhere unless the lady decided that it would. He himself suspected that Stella knew more than she would ever say. Though how much more was imponderable.

"And the boy—his son?" said Rupert.

"They took him to Casselton General, suffering from what they believed to be traumatic amnesia caused by his witnessing the crash."

"Do *you* believe it was?"

"I am no medical expert," said Stella. "I have no beliefs one way or the other."

"Then what?" said Rupert, pressing on.

"I visited. I tried to bring him home to Belthorp for Christmas, but he wasn't well enough to come."

"In what way was he not well enough?"

Stella remembered the strange words Thomas had screamed at her and the strange voice that appeared to possess him like some sort of alien spirit. She shivered inwardly.

"I do not know why he was not well enough," she said with apparent calm. "As I said, I have no medical knowledge whatsoever. You should go and see Dr. Ramsay."

"We already have done," said the inspector. "He has, as you will appreciate, been interviewed several times by various people. It was from his care that Thomas was apparently taken in the middle of the night."

"And his father's sheepskin coat was left behind on

the bed," said Rupert. "We know it was the same coat as that from which the strip on the tanker's wheel was torn. That is a firm connection."

"Yes," said Stella. "I thought that was odd too."

She expected to be asked her opinion again and was rather taken aback by Rupert's next line of questioning.

"On this Monday morning after the boy disappeared, you went to the hospital to see him. You were shocked when they showed you the coat and told you what had happened?"

"Yes," said Stella guardedly. "I was. Anybody would be."

She looked hard at Inspector Galway and said pointedly, "I was also amazed that the hospital failed to inform me of the situation when I rang the ward on Sunday."

Rupert was impatient to return to his own line of questioning. He ignored Stella's barbed complaint. After all, it was of no concern to him.

"But the words you were heard to say then were a puzzle," he said.

"I don't remember what I said," said Stella, but she was lying.

The man from the ministry looked at his notebook.

"We have witnesses who heard you say, and I quote, 'My God, it must all have been true.' What did you mean by that?"

Stella took a deep breath and fixed her interlocutor with a penetrating gaze. Her amber eyes darkened as the pupils dilated.

"I cannot remember saying those words, so I cannot possibly tell you what they mean. I must have been misheard, or perhaps I was simply confused."

Both men knew that she was not speaking the truth. But there was nothing they could do about it. And one of them was really rather pleased, even if it did mean that the mystery was nowhere nearer to being solved.

"So what do you think happened to the boy and his father?" persisted Rupert.

"They went out of my life," said Stella sharply. "When my husband died, I thought I could never be hurt again. What happened just three weeks ago is like another bereavement. Please give me leave to mourn."

John Galway leant over and put one hand gently on her arm.

"What did you do after you left the hospital that day?" said Rupert, ignoring her last answer entirely. The inspector looked across at him, appalled at such callousness.

"I went into St. Mary's," said Stella coldly.

"The cathedral?"

"It is where I go when I am at a loss for an answer. There is someone there that I can talk to."

"A priest?" said Rupert, Biro poised, ready to write down a name.

John Galway suppressed a laugh.

Even Stella was drawn to smile.

"Someone rather more important than that," she said.

Rupert flushed as he realized what she meant.

"And did you get an answer?" he said rather spitefully.

Inspector Galway stood up abruptly, appalled at the man's rudeness and determined to dissociate himself from it. It was surely time to go!

Stella smiled faintly.

"Life's not a textbook with all the answers in the back," she said. "I think you probably know that."

"Yes," sighed Rupert, putting his pen and book away in his breast pocket. The interview was clearly over.

# CHAPTER 10

# Saturday in York

Alison left home ahead of Nesta. She was about to suggest their going together, to ask where and when she had arranged to meet Amy. Then she held back, thinking that perhaps they both needed time apart. So she went alone for the early bus, knowing that Nesta would be at least half an hour behind her.

The bus ride was a pleasant one, taking her through neat suburbia and past fields where in summer cattle grazed, into the heart of the great walled city. She had sight of the narrow streets of the old town and the minster that towered above them. This had been her home for fourteen years, and fourteen years is a long time in anyone's language.

She got off at Piccadilly and wandered quite aimlessly from shop to shop; bought a new lipstick in

Boots, then thought about taking it with her to Ormingat. It was a shiver of a thought, a self-tormenting shiver, such as one feels when an idea slips away and does not know how to put itself into words. The center of York at noon on Saturday was so divorced from any inkling of space travel. Even in midwinter, the streets were busy. In fact, they were busier today than on any day since Christmas. The English weather had done one of its brilliant back-flips. The sun was shining, and the air was mild and balmy.

She had no need to shop, nothing much to shop for now that she was about to leave this Earth. What should she buy? A book for the journey . . .

The thought seemed ludicrous, as if she were going somewhere by train. *The train for Ormingat will be leaving from platform 12 in five minutes.*

Alison spent nearly an hour in the bookshop in Davygate, drinking coffee and then browsing over the books in a shop that had become one of her favorite places. She eventually came out with a copy of *Dombey and Son,* one of the few Dickens novels she had not read so far, and an assortment of paperbacks, on offer at three for the price of two. There would be plenty of time after all—to read, and reread!

Alison walked round till she came within sight of the minster. She looked up and down the familiar streets. *I don't want to live worlds away from here.* On the three-year journey home, she knew she would cease to feel like this; she would come to cherish the thought of Ormingat, her birthplace and the beloved land of her childhood, but not yet.

Coming out of Marks and Spencer's, where she had bought some salad and a cake for Sunday tea, she ran into Mrs. Jolly, who lived next door at number 10.

"Better weather, this," said her neighbor, beaming as if she had produced the sunshine by her own efforts. "You never know how it's going to be. Two-faced January, my late husband used to call it, something to do with Janus looking both ways. Well, I am sure it's very two-faced about the weather, snow, frost, and flood, and now look at it! It could be April!"

"Well, let's hope it stays this way!" said Alison, smiling and anxious to move on. Mrs. Jolly was always a great one for talking! They parted, and Alison walked a little faster for a while to make it look as if she were indeed pressed for time. Mrs. Jolly was headed in the direction of Piccadilly. Alison quickly decided to go in the opposite direction to make for the railway station and get the bus home from there. It was not that she disliked her neighbor's company. But today was not the day for it!

In St. Sampson's Square Nesta and Amy sat in the sunshine, their mission accomplished. Only the leafless trees betrayed the fact that it was still the middle of winter.

The girls had spent an hour or more in Coppergate, mainly window-shopping, and then they had wandered round the town streets deep in conversation, though it was Amy who did most of the talking. Nesta was trying to hide her feelings, and whilst they were on the move she could just about manage it. By the time they came to the square, the morning was over and they were feeling quite hungry. They sat down to consider where to go next.

The new hockey boots were in a green plastic bag on the seat between them. Amy was looking forward to being on the new team, playing at the back and fiercely guarding the goal. Thoughts of it rambled on in her head, and what she said when she spoke made sense to her, though not to Nesta.

"She's changed, you know. She's like a different person."

"Who?" said Nesta, roused from her own daydreams. "What *are* you talking about?"

Amy laughed.

"Sorry," she said. "You can't read my thoughts. My mum says I'm always doing that! Amanda Watkins has changed. Now she's organizing the junior hockey team. She's turned quite nice."

Nesta shrugged her shoulders.

"She's been thinking of asking you to play midfield because you're the best runner. But—I know this sounds odd after what happened—she seems shy of asking you. She wanted me to find out if you were interested. Not that I'd blame you if you weren't."

Nesta gave Amy a look of such absolute misery that her friend was immediately alarmed. She wished she had not mentioned Amanda.

"It's not important," she said hurriedly. "If it still hurts, you don't need have anything to do with her. Only you don't mind me being on the team, do you?"

Amy looked at Nesta anxiously. Loyalty was her watchword.

"If you do mind," she added, "I won't join in. It's just a game, after all."

"It's not that," said Nesta quickly. "It's something else altogether. Nothing to do with school."

"Tell me then," said Amy. "It can't be all that bad. Surely it can't."

"It can," said Nesta miserably. "It is. It's terrible, but I can't tell you anything about it."

"Nesta Gwynn!" said Amy, bringing both fists down on the bag that held the hockey boots. "You can tell me anything. I am your best friend, aren't I?"

"You are my best friend, Amy. And you always will be, no matter what. But I can't tell you. I really can't."

"It's best to tell, no matter what it is," said Amy. "Remember the bullying. When I told about that, it was all put right. It even helped Amanda, I think. She's a much better person now."

"It's not as simple as that," said Nesta. "I wish it were.

It's just we might be moving away soon. My parents might have to go back to Boston. And I don't want to go. I'd love to be on the team, only I might not be here long enough."

Before Amy could ask any questions, Nesta caught sight of her mother coming up Parliament Street toward where they were sitting.

"Look," she said, as brightly as she could, "there's my mom. Let's ask her to take us to Betty's for lunch. She offered to this morning. But mind you don't say anything about us going away. We're not even sure to be going. It could be called off. And it's supposed to be a secret."

They both stood up and waved hard at Alison, who soon saw them, waved back, and came to meet them.

"Come on then, you two," she said as she drew near. "Time for eats. I said this morning I would take you to Betty's. I guess you'd be pleased to take up the offer now!"

Afterward, on the bus home, Alison said anxiously, "You didn't tell Amy anything, did you?"

"No, Mom, not really," said Nesta, looking not at her mother but out of the window at the Museum Gardens. "I did say we might be moving away from here, but not where or when, and certainly not how. There's no need, you know, to warn me not to tell. Most of it is untellable."

# CHAPTER 11

# Matthew's Return

In the twilight, something silvery, like a winter moth, flitted across the back lawn at number 8 Linden Drive. The presence settled lightly in the corner of the open porch. Then, with a swift shimmer, it rippled into full life and became Matthew Gwynn. The glass in each of the side windows vibrated. Matthew caught his breath and rested a moment against the house door. It was locked and there was no light from the kitchen.

Matthew tapped several times, urgently but not too loudly. No one came. He stood back onto the lawn and looked at all of the windows he could see, but there was no light in any of them. Looking at his watch, he saw that it was a quarter to five. He walked round to the front of the house, past the wall of a hedge that protected the property of the Marwoods at number 6.

He could not see their garden through the dense, high evergreens; more important, no one on the other side would be able to see him. At that moment, in his sweatshirt and jeans, possibly locked out of his own house, he felt self-conscious.

There were no lights at the front of the house either. No one home. And he had no key to get in. He strolled casually down the front path to the gate and looked toward the end of the street where the bus would stop. A bus did stop.

Coming toward him, shopping in either hand, was Mrs. Jolly.

"Afternoon, Mr. Gwynn," she said as she approached. "Just seen your wife in town. Been a nice day, hasn't it?"

As she drew closer, she saw something that Matthew had not observed. His hands were covered in slimy vegetation.

"You been having trouble with that pond of yours?" said Mrs. Jolly. "Saw you'd been draining it."

"Yes," said Matthew, rubbing his hand on an oil rag he managed to find in his jeans pocket. "There's a blockage somewhere."

"Never did like garden ponds," said Mrs. Jolly. "They're always a nuisance. You're forever having to do something with them. Either they dry up, or they smell, or they flood the garden. I'd get rid of it if I were you."

Matthew smiled sheepishly.

"It was there when we came to live here," he said. "I suppose it's part of the character of the house. It might even be on top of an old well. I know we always find it easy to fill."

"Never thought of that," said Mrs. Jolly, looking cautious. "Probably best left, then. Let sleeping dogs lie."

It did just occur to her that a dammed-up well next door might send the water to other properties: water always finds somewhere to go.

She walked on up to her own gate and waved cheerio.

*At least she didn't mention the frog,* thought Matthew gratefully.

The problem was what to do next. He walked round to the side of the house and contemplated the Marwoods' hedge for some minutes. The next bus would arrive in about half an hour. He couldn't stay skulking by the hedge for long. Standing in the back garden, he might be observed. Paranoia maybe, but Mrs. Jolly was never far from a window. A mist was coming up; the weather was on the change again. Matthew looked up and down the street and decided to spend the time walking the long way round to the bus stop.

So he went out of the path and walked quite slowly, head down, toward the crescent at the opposite end from the main road. A gentle walk, all he felt capable of after the shock to the system that always attended the process of diminishing and increasing, would give time for the next bus to arrive. There was no one in sight. The mist thickened and he was glad of it.

The bus passed by on the main road and stopped just a few yards ahead of him. He was relieved to see Alison and Nesta alight from it.

"Allie!" he called. "Nesta!"

They turned, startled.

"It's Dad," said Nesta. "What's he doing here?"

For one hysterical moment Alison thought that the spaceship must have moved somehow. Then Matthew reached them and said breathlessly, "I'm locked out. I didn't have my key with me."

Nesta flung her arms round her father and sobbed.

"You're safe," she said. "I thought we might never see you again!"

Alison looked round anxiously to make sure there were no passersby. There weren't.

"It's all right," she said. "Calm down now. We can talk about it when we get into the house."

She turned them both round and set them off in the right direction.

"You should have stayed on the back porch, Mattie," she said, shaking her head with a sort of motherly exasperation. "You might have known we wouldn't be long."

Matthew didn't bother to explain about Mrs. Jolly and the pond. It could only complicate things.

Once indoors, they all felt a need to draw breath. Matthew was still suffering the after-effects of diminishing and increasing in such a short space of time. Nesta was once again shocked and bewildered. To see her father emerging from the mist and running toward them had been almost like seeing a ghost. The calmest was Alison. The other two sat tensely silent as she put away the shopping and boiled the kettle to make them all a strong cup of Yorkshire tea.

*Bostonians from Ormingat, settling down to a reviving British cuppa,* she thought wryly. *We really are confused!*

## CHAPTER 12

# Fresh Instructions

The house the Gwynns had "inherited" had come to them complete with rather old-fashioned, comfortable furniture. Over the years they had made few changes. In this respect, perhaps they demonstrated that, deep down, they continued to feel that they were just visitors to the planet with no absolute right to place or property. To Nesta, on the other hand, this lack of change had always been reassuring.

*But we're really Americans, aren't we? And you and Daddy came from Boston.*

Nesta was sitting in the big green armchair, automatically drinking the tea her mother had handed her, and those were the thoughts that came uppermost to her mind. The old green leather armchair was somehow linked to eternity. Ormingat was in the province of the elves and the shoemaker.

Matthew was about to speak but Nesta spoke first. She brushed her fine hair back from her brow, leant forward, and said, "What is it like?"

Matthew smiled back at her.

"Not so bad," he said. "I mean, it's like going very fast down a steep chute. You feel a bit dazed afterward. I'm still rather light-headed, but it soon wears off. You don't really know that you have changed size at all because you are always the same to yourself."

"No, Dad," said Nesta impatiently. "That's not what I am talking about. What is it like inside this ship? What does it look like? How would you manage to live there for three years? It *was* three years you said the journey took?"

"Round about that," said Matthew. "But have no worry on that score. The ship is clearly split into two hemispheres. In one, there is spacious living accommodation in the style of Earth. In fact, our quarters don't look vastly different from the rooms in this house."

"But three years confined like that! Even if it *is* comfortable, it must be very strange. Like being in prison."

"Not really," said Alison, speaking as a researcher recalling some academic fact. "There is so much to see and do. Then there are periods of suspension that can last for much longer than sleep on Earth. We go away into ourselves and return revived."

Nesta put her face in her hands and tried desperately to make some sense of what her parents were saying. She tried to reach their level of calm, though her mind was saying, *This can't be true.* She almost felt as if she were playing along with some grotesque pretense. But she knew she had seen Matthew diminish, and nothing could alter that. The memory not only frightened her; it made her feel physically sick.

"And what about the other hemisphere?" she said at length. "You said there were two."

"The other," said her father slowly, "is pure Ormingat. It is a space laboratory such as you have never seen, not even in the most sci-fi of sci-fi movies. I am not even sure that I can explain it to you properly. Separate *space* and *laboratory*. Think of the space as an area restful, flowing, and beautiful. And the laboratory is all illusion. What needs to appear appears. The illusions come and go, like tides ebbing and flowing. Two things there remain fixed. At a height above, so that you raise your head to look at it, there is a communications cube that glows and speaks. On the base of the laboratory, so that you must look far down, is something like the dial of a clock, midnight blue and set with jewels like stars in the sky. Other lights circle it with what looks like no sort of order, but gradually they will fall in line and that will be the moment of takeoff. Such is the mechanism that eventually will act as a trigger to detonate the rockets that send the ship back into space. It was set to reach its critical point at the exact moment we were meant to leave Earth. I check the setting every year. Last June, it had six and a half Earth years to go before every one of its eighty lights would join in a line to form the arrow. Each light represents a quarter of a year."

"And the rockets cannot be detonated till that moment, fixed from the outset by those who know how the clock runs—which we don't. So for us to leave before our time is impossible," said Alison, seeing this as a definite cause for delay. There were reasons, strong reasons, for wanting to go; there were reasons, stronger reasons, for hoping to stay till the proper and appointed time.

Matthew smiled. Already the thought of returning to his own planet was a tingle of excitement in his soul.

"We don't have to wait. The years have melted and blended. The communicator has given us a new return date. And I have checked it against the clock. We have just seven days before the ship's main rocket detonates."

He looked at Nesta and reached across and gripped her hand.

"You cannot realize how wonderful that is!"

Nesta drew back.

"Of course she can't," said Alison sharply. "She was born here. She needs time to get used to the idea. A week is far too little. We were to tell her next year. She was meant to have five years of knowing. This is unfair."

Nesta's face went white. Her mind was searching about for lucid thoughts.

"So what do we do for the week? How do we live through it, knowing?"

"It won't be a week just waiting," said her father. "We enter the ship four days from now. On Wednesday, at sunset, we leave this house never to return. We settle into our new quarters ready for the journey to begin."

Alison was watching her daughter's face, seeing the terror that was below the surface.

"Enough, Mattie," she said. "I think we have had enough for one night."

When Alison went to say good night to Nesta, now tucked up in bed and longing to find oblivion in sleep, she leant over her and said softly, "Don't worry, my darling. Don't dwell on thoughts of rockets and detonators. Love is a fuel that goes a lot further. Wherever we are, we are together."

She turned out the light, stood briefly in the doorway, and found herself whispering, *"Nallytan, Neshayla ban,"* words that had fallen into disuse in these latter years. Then in her too, as in Mattie, something of excitement stirred. *I am not American after all. I am not a true member of this muddled, restless Earth.*

# CHAPTER 13

# Sunday

The next day being Sunday, they went to church. That was part of their routine, an ambiguous sort of "religious observation." They were meant to steep themselves in every aspect of human life, but this was not just empty ritual: God was not mocked.

The Gwynns did not go to churches in their own neighborhood. They worshipped in the larger churches and cathedrals within driving distance. They did not discriminate between the different branches of the Christian church. It still puzzled them that there should be so many. They would also have happily attended synagogue, mosque, or temple, but their New England background left them too ignorant to know what to do when they got there; and it was always essential that they should blend in unobtrusively. Their

Boston memories of the church in Copley Square might have made them strict Episcopalians, but their own faith, the faith of Ormingat, was a birthright that went deeper than any implanted memory.

In the minster that morning each of the Gwynns was wrapped in individual thought. Matthew looked up at the stained-glass windows, wonders of art, telling their stories, expressing their faith. *This place is beautiful, but so is Ormingat. This place is godly, but the world round it fails. In Ormingat there is too much love for there to be such failure. Arish inghlat, Argule.*

Alison kept head down and hands clasped, deep in meditation that was not quite prayer. *We all die someday. Where we die is not important. We are all souls in the same small universe. Deep inside me I do have a yearning for Ormingat, where my own life began; but Nesta's life began here. She is distraught and bewildered. I feel her pain and I can hardly bear it. Entesh, Argule, entesh.*

Nesta sat back in place, head scarcely bowed. Her eyes were open but seeing nothing. The minster, the priest, and the people might as well have been inaudible and invisible. Her thoughts were too busy elsewhere, shying away from questions to which she could never hope to find answers. *I don't want to go. Help me find some way out. I am not a coward. Even when I let them bully me at school, it wasn't because I was afraid. It was that I felt ashamed of being different. This is worse. I am different. I will always be different. Please, God, help me.*

They drove home in silence.

Alison prepared what she now thought of as her last Sunday lunch on Earth. Matthew peeled the potatoes and the turnip. Alison took the roast out of the oven, put in the Yorkshire pudding, and then made the gravy.

"Odd that we'll never do this again," she said, gesturing to the pans on top of the cooker.

"There'll be similar things to do," said Matthew. "Ormingat will not be so very different in material respects."

"A change of menu?" said Alison with a wry smile.

"I don't know," said Matthew, shaking his head at her. "You know I don't. But you do know exactly what I mean."

Nesta had gone straight to her own room after church, and was busy finishing her French homework. It was as if she were operating on different levels: double-booking the whole of her life. *I can be in two places at once. Miss Simpson will expect my French translation to be handed in first thing tomorrow morning. If the world is going to end on Wednesday, I must still know how to conjugate* avoir *and* être.

"Nesta," her mother called up the stairs. "Lunch in five minutes."

"Okay, Mom. I'm coming."

"I know we need to talk," said Matthew as they sat at the table, "but let's be like the English. Let's enjoy our meal first and think of less important things. Have you finished your homework, Nesta?"

"Yes, Dad, I have. And if you don't think *that* is important, you should talk to Miss Simpson!"

It was a shaky attempt at a joke. She really felt more like crying. Eating was difficult too, persuading her teeth to chew and her throat to swallow. *I don't want to be in this situation. I want everything to be back to normal.*

When the meal was over and the table cleared, they went into the front room. A wall light was lit either side of the hearth; the gas fire glowed in the grate. This was the coffee-and-biscuits room. This was the place for an afternoon nap. The television in the corner was only ever switched on in the evening.

"Now," said Matthew. "I shall give you as much as I know of the details of our departure. It would really have been better if you had gone into the ship, Allie. You are so much better than I am at remembering things."

Earth convention had given the job to Matthew from the first. Occasionally, in the early days, Alison had entered the spaceship; but after Nesta's birth it became mostly impractical. Earth convention is much more tolerant of the father going off on "business trips."

"Take it slowly," said Alison. "We can ask you questions if you seem to leave anything out."

"Well, in the first place, we enter the spaceship on Wednesday—you first, then Nesta, and I go last. The house has to be left tidy and locked up but there is no need for us to take anything with us. We are allowed to fill a bag each with things we might really value—books, photographs, and suchlike."

From the floor beside him, he picked up a yellow tube-shaped bag with canvas handles and a zip round one end for the opening. It was one of three. They looked quite ordinary and earthly. For the past five years they had been stored away on the top shelf of a wardrobe—Matthew had been given them on one of his yearly trips—a new piece of equipment specially adapted to store permitted Earth objects. Ormingat science never stands still.

"I was given these bags for the purpose. They are more capacious than they look. They will diminish with us and we shall carry them aboard."

"And we go," said Alison, "just like that? What about the bank? What about Professor Leonard? I am supposed to be working for him on Thursday afternoon. Don't we give some sort of notice?"

"Not necessary," said Matthew. "It will all be taken care of by others who will see to the house and create whatever cover story they feel is needed. Not our job. You know the power of Ormingat. Illusions can be easily created."

Alison was still not happy. For the past seven years she had worked as a research assistant at the university, part-time work, poorly paid, but enormously satisfying.

Matthew saw the look on her face and said grudgingly, "I suppose if you feel strongly about it, you could send the professor a note."

To leave at such short notice was unnerving. Alison had become used to her practical Earth persona. Minds and bodies interact: Alison was neat, her dark curly hair never out of place, her clothes always spotless. The deep brown eyes shone with human intelligence of a strictly logical sort. It was a personality not easily set aside.

"Is this haste necessary?" she asked. "Is it such an emergency?"

"They seem to think it is."

He looked warily toward Nesta. The Ormingatra advisers clearly thought she represented a risk and must be taken out of danger as soon as possible. He was reluctant to explain in her presence that she was the chief reason for their going so soon. The thought, however, made him take another decision.

"I think perhaps you shouldn't go to school tomorrow after all," he said to her as lightly as he could. "So you needn't worry about that homework. You won't be going back."

"I am not worried about the homework," said Nesta in quiet fury. "It is finished. I have finished it. I just told you I had. What's more, I am quite proud of it. It's neat and tidy and ten-out-of-ten correct."

"I know it is, honey," said Matthew. "Let's not get into a muddle. All I am saying is that tomorrow you needn't go to school. It would probably be better if you didn't."

"I am going to school, Dad," said Nesta through clenched teeth. "I am going to school whether you like it or not."

"Let her be, Matt," said Alison. "It will do no harm for her to go. She won't tell anyone anything. She's got more sense. And if she's hanging round here for three days, she'll only feel worse and be bored."

"So what are you suggesting?" said Matthew. "We let her go to school till Wednesday and come home that afternoon ready to embark?"

"Just that," said Alison. "And I shall continue with my work on the great explorers on Tuesday. I have nothing lined up for Wednesday and I shall keep it that way. And you must make a sensible excuse to the bank that lets you finish on Tuesday afternoon. Tell them you have to go back to Boston for family reasons. Ask for a month's furlough. Anything. But don't leave it up to Ormingat to do everything. I know they can, but we want to do things our own way."

Nesta nodded agreement. The less they left up to that alien planet, the more chance it seemed to her there was of not going there at all.

"Very well," said Matthew, "you can do things your way. My way is to let our people take care of everything. I'll tell the bank no lies. I'll work till Wednesday.

Then I'll just disappear. My vanishing will be covered one way or another. It's none of my business."

They left it at that. They were not a family accustomed to arguing. Which made the argument next day all the harder to bear.

That evening the rain came down again. There was a scramble to return the frog to its lily pad, something they had forgotten in all the stress. They worked in darkness and in near silence. Nesta stayed indoors. There was no laughter and no fun.

# CHAPTER 14

# Monday at School

"Come out, come out, wherever you are," said Mr. Telford in a singsong voice.

It was to Nesta these words were playfully addressed. Mr. Telford had asked her to read. She was not looking out the window, or talking or doing anything wrong at all. She even seemed to be paying attention, but all the words in the book and all the words that were being spoken as part of the lesson were passing her by unobserved.

"Come on, Nesta," said Mr. Telford, a little less patiently, "read the next paragraph—'One evening just before the new moon was due . . .' Do get a move on."

Nesta came out of her thoughts, blushed, and gave Mr. Telford a nervous smile. She had lost her place and didn't know where to begin.

"Page forty, fifth line down. I hope you'll decide to stay with us for the rest of the lesson. I won't ask you where you've been," said the teacher. Nesta was one of his best pupils. This aberration was unusual.

With an effort, Nesta read the next page and was relieved when told she could stop. Mr. Telford made no further comment on her inattention. It was as well the lesson was English and not history with the sharp-tongued Mr. Fielder. If he had come out with the usual, caustic "Which planet are you from?" or even "Welcome to this world!" it might have been more than Nesta could bear.

 At break, Amy was quick to ask her what was wrong.

"I lost the place, that's all," said Nesta. "I was just thinking about something."

"But you look worried, Nesta," said Amy. "I know you by now. I don't know why you have to hide it when people upset you. It's always much better to tell. Is it the same as what was upsetting you on Saturday? Do you know you're going now?"

Nesta desperately wanted to tell Amy everything, but *everything* would have been incredible, and *nearly* everything might be dangerous. *I can't tell her we are leaving on Wednesday. I can't really tell her very much at all.*

"I don't know when we are going," she said, "but it seems pretty certain that we are. And I honestly don't want to go at all. But I'm not even thirteen till next month; so I have no choice."

"In that case," said Amy, "I suppose you'll just have to get used to the idea. I don't want you to go—and I will really miss you. But things like that can't be helped. Remember Lucinda McNeil—she went to live in Greece. At least you won't have a new language to learn."

It was all Nesta could do not to cry. *Compared to where I am going, Greece is just next door.* And what was the language of Ormingat? Strange sounds made by that boy in his hospital bed, eerie sounds not of this Earth!

Amy looked at her woebegone expression and said, "If you are really so unhappy about it, why don't you ask your parents not to go? That's the only way you'd be able to stay."

"I can't," said Nesta. "Don't ask me why. I just can't."

In saying that, she suddenly realized that she would never be able to tell anyone the complete truth ever again. She could not even talk to her parents properly anymore. The secret they had hidden from her for years, in which she was now included, did not bring them closer together. It drove them apart. *I can't trust them. I still love them, but in some strange way I almost hate them too. Is it possible to love and hate the same people?*

The bus was late. The rain came on in a steady light drizzle. Nesta didn't bother to take out her umbrella. She just stood waiting and stoically enduring the damp and the cold. Ormingat might have wonderful weather but that did not seem a particularly compelling attraction. *Stuff your wonderful weather, Organmat,* she thought, deliberately and bitterly distorting the name of the one that James Martin had given. *This is Earth and I am of Earth!*

When she eventually reached home, it was almost dark and her mother was waiting at the bus stop under a big golf umbrella. Alison was relieved to see her daughter alight from the bus. Nesta's clothes were soaked and her fine hair was so wet that strands of it were clinging to her cheeks.

"I thought the bus would be late," said Alison. "It's been on the local news about the traffic. I guessed you might have forgotten your umbrella. And I wasn't wrong. You look half-drowned!"

"I didn't forget my umbrella," said Nesta with a hint of aggression in her voice. "It's in my bag. I couldn't be bothered to get it out. There's not much I can be bothered with today."

They walked along the street in silence after that. Alison held the umbrella over the two of them. Nesta did not object. She kept her head down, looking at the pavement, making no effort to avoid any puddles. But, whatever it might appear to be, this was not adolescent rebellion. The feelings Nesta was harboring were mature and terrible.

"Go and get changed," said her mother as they

entered the house. "And dry your hair. You don't want to catch pneumonia, do you?"

"I wouldn't much care," said Nesta dourly. "Do germs diminish? Or will I be put into quarantine?"

"We shall all have three years of quarantine," said her mother, "if you think of it that way. And there are wonderful treatments for all Earth's ills in the ship's medicine cabinet. But I would rather you stayed healthy."

As Nesta went up the stairs, she turned back and looked down at her mother. She had come to a decision. She would not ask them to stay. It could, if they liked, be a one-sided conversation. She would simply inform them that she was not going. It would be their job to sort it out.

"I want to talk to you when I come down," she said. "No stopping for tea or trying to be ultra-English. I want to talk straightaway to you and to Dad."

Alison nodded.

"Talking would be best," she said. "We do love you. Please don't hate us."

It was not what Nesta expected her mother to say. It seemed uncomfortably perceptive.

# CHAPTER 15

# The Man from the Ministry

After his visit to Mrs. Dalrymple's, Rupert Shawcross was not satisfied. He knew she was hiding something and he couldn't fathom what it could be.

Back in Casselton, he looked around, saw some minor signs of change, but was pleased to see that the town was easily recognizable between visits. He left Inspector Galway at the police station and took a bus to Ferndale, an estate of bungalows that looked like toy town. At number 6 Pennington Close lived a cousin of his, a schoolteacher whom he had seen twice or maybe three times in the past five years. Normally it was she who looked in on him if she happened to be in Manchester.

"Well, this is a surprise, Rupert," she said. "It must be ten years or more since you came this far north.

Business, pleasure, or has somebody died that I don't know about?"

Audrey always took a mocking tone with her cousin. He seemed to her to be stiff and pompous, but not bad really. He did not resent being made fun of; he was simply puzzled by it.

"Business," he said, "but not business I can readily discuss. You understand?"

"All very hush-hush then, is it?" she said. "Time for a cup of tea?"

"Yes, please," said Rupert gladly, knowing that the tea would be accompanied by cakes and sandwiches. They had been childhood friends as well as cousins. That is something that never gets lost. "There *is* something you might be able to help me with. I can't give you any details, of course, but we are trying to trace a missing child. I have spoken to the woman who used to look after him, before he and his father set off for who knows where, and I feel sure she is covering something up."

"Not *the* missing child?" said Audrey promptly. "The one who disappeared from Casselton General? How on earth does it concern you? I thought you were a government department, interested in international drug barons and that sort of thing."

"That sort of thing," mumbled Rupert as he chewed his sandwich.

"No leads?"

"Not really, but we are thinking that the boy may have given something away before the accident—told someone something that might give us a clue. Only it's hard to know whom to ask."

"Ask his teacher," said Audrey promptly. "She'll be able to tell you who his best friend is. If he had a secret, the best friend is surely the one he could trust. All kids have their cronies."

That was a dangerous suggestion! In Belthorp lived Mickey Trent, Thomas Tonitheen's best friend. Mickey was one of the only two people on the planet who knew the truth about the Derwents. Rupert had got nowhere in his questioning of Stella Dalrymple. Might he fare better with an innocent child?

Rupert tried to get a visit arranged the next day but the school was closed—teachers on a training course. So he had to be content to wait till Monday to check out the school in Belthorp. Friday was not allowed to lie fallow, however. There was this boy, James Martin, living right here in Casselton. The boy, by his own account, had known Thomas Derwent for no more than two days. It was a slim chance, but better than doing nothing.

It was quite dark, though still reasonably early, when Rupert reached the house in Hedley Crescent where James lived with his dad and mam and younger brother and sister. It was six-year-old Carla who opened the door, followed by her mother and a white dog that might have been distantly related to a smooth-haired terrier.

"Yes?" said Mrs. Martin sharply, holding on to the dog by its collar and pushing Carla behind her. "What do you want? I've got all the double glazing I need and I don't wish to buy anything."

Calypso, the dog, struggled to be free. She did not bark. She just wriggled.

"I wonder if you'd mind, Mrs. Martin—it is Mrs. Martin?—letting me have a word with young James?"

"I most certainly would," said his mother. "I don't even know who you are. And I think I should point out to you that this dog does not bark; but she bites quite hard if strangers attempt to cross the doorstep uninvited."

Rupert fumbled in his pocket for identification.

"This is official business," he said. "We are concerned about the disappearance of Thomas Derwent. You will appreciate that we don't take such disappearances lightly. If your son disappeared, just think how you would feel."

"I would feel desperate," said Mrs. Martin, "but that doesn't alter the fact that Jamie can tell you nothing. I only wish he had had the sense not to write to the paper about it. He's too clever by half."

"That's just what we need," said Rupert smiling, "the evidence of a clever and observant boy."

At that moment Jamie came up the garden path, his schoolbag slung on his back and a half-eaten packet of crisps in his hand. Calypso wagged her tail frantically but remained silent. Mrs. Martin swooped on the crisps and said, "How many times have I told you! Get in and wash your hands. Your tea's keeping warm in the oven. Why do you have to dawdle your way home?"

"This must be James," said Rupert quickly. "My name's Rupert Shawcross, James. I am one of the people looking into the disappearance of your friend Tonitheen."

He put out his hand to shake Jamie's but, flattered though he was, Jamie knew condescension when he met it. He thrust his own hands deep into his jacket pockets.

"I told all I knew in the letter to *The Courier*," he said. "I suppose that's why you're here."

"You mentioned in that letter that you would be willing to help him anytime he needed you. Has he been in touch? Has he asked you for help?"

Jamie gave him a look of contempt.

"I don't want to answer any questions," he said. "I think you should go away. Our dog doesn't bark, but she sometimes bites, especially if she doesn't like visitors."

"That's what I told him," said his mother. "Now go upstairs and get washed. It's too cold to be standing out here."

Jamie turned his back on the stranger.

Rupert, undeterred, called after him. "If Tonitheen does put in an appearance, you must let us know immediately. I'll leave my card and telephone number with your mother."

Calypso at this point managed to break free and shot back into the house out of the cold and the dark. She was an animal very fond of her creature comforts.

# CHAPTER 16

# I'm Not Going

"I'm not going," said Nesta vehemently, "and nothing you say will make me."

The Gwynns were together in the sitting room. Matthew and Alison sat in the armchairs either side of the hearth. Nesta was sharing the settee with Charlie, the sleek black cat, and a fluffy-dog pajama case called Percy.

She sat up very straight and stared not at either parent but at the flames of the gas fire. She had said her say. Now it was their turn.

It was her mother who spoke first.

"There's not really a choice, you know," she said quite gently. "You are who you are. Deep down, you must have always known that you were special."

Nesta frowned but said nothing. The truth of the re-mark made her shiver.

"Your father was given some of the background to our situation when he went into the ship. It appears that only two Ormingat children have ever been born here on Earth and entwined with the home planet," her mother went on. "You are one of them. You were part of the reason why the child Tonitheen was sent here. The Ormingat scientists needed a 'control': they wanted to know whether an earthborn child would be any different from a child born on Ormingat and spending his formative years on Earth. Things, as you know, went wrong when the boy and his father were in-volved in that accident. Now caution has made our re-turn home an imperative."

"It's not *my* home," said Nesta sharply. "My home is here, where I was born and have always lived."

"That is how you feel now," said Alison. "But your deepest being truly does belong to Ormingat, and when we get there you will recognize it immediately."

At that moment, Nesta found herself remembering her mother's fairy-tale description of the Faraway Planet, and she did not like it. She could not believe in those swirly soft towers and misty gates. It sounded too sickly sweet for words.

"I don't *want* to go there," said Nesta. "I don't *want* to live in your marshmallow world. Earth is real. Or-mingat sounds to me like a pathetic fairy story."

Charlie, upset at the argumentative sound of Nesta's voice, jumped down and slunk into the corner beneath the television set.

Matthew had sat silently listening. It seemed to him that Alison was not making the point very well. The old story was meant as a link, not an explanation.

"We must tell her the truth," he said, leaning forward in his chair and looking earnestly from one to the other. "She is right. She is much too old for fairy tales."

Alison was startled.

"What is the truth?" she said. "Do we know it?"

"We know what we know," said Matthew firmly. "And that has to be enough."

"Well, you tell, Mattie," said Alison. "I wouldn't know how to start."

"We must start from what we really do know," said Matthew, "what is incontrovertible fact."

Nesta gave her father a much kinder look than she had been able to give her mother. She knew absolutely that there were missing pieces in this jigsaw and she wanted them found and fitted into place.

"Let's begin with what *you* know, Nesta. You saw me disappear into the center of the pond on Friday. You saw it with your own eyes and you were understandably shocked."

Nesta nodded miserably.

"When I went down into the ground, I entered the

spaceship and it was exactly as I have described it. There I talked to a screen that glowed green whenever it spoke back to me. It spoke in English, because for the time I am on Earth I am an English speaker. My memory of the language of Ormingat is very hazy. A few phrases remain, and they are the voice of Ormingat, a voice I see disturbs you when I give the planet's name its proper sound. When you say *Ormingat,* it comes out as an English word, with English intonation. When I say it, there is a sort of resonance that does not belong here. *Ormingat.*"

He said the word slowly and deliberately, smiling at his daughter as he did so.

*"Ormeen-in-ghat,"* said Nesta, trying and failing to get the right vibration.

She frowned.

"How can I learn a whole new language when I cannot even manage to say one word correctly?"

"The body changes on the journey home, and the different atmosphere on our planet when we get there makes it all possible. On Ormingat, you will forget all but a residue of Earth words and accents."

"Then I would stop being me," said Nesta harshly.

"No, sweetheart," said her father, "that could never happen. You are your wonderful self forever, wherever you may be. Just let me continue. This time when I visited the spaceship, it was to sort out the matter of returning home. On my normal visits, I have taken the research your mother and I have worked on year in, year out since we came here, under the guise afforded us by the human work we do."

"That sounds like cheating," said Nesta.

"Not really," said Matthew. "Our motives are pure. For us, knowledge is an end in itself."

"Then you should stay here and go on studying," said Nesta sulkily. "That would save us all a lot of bother."

"Yes," said her father, "but we can't, and since we can't we must accept and even welcome what we must do instead. In two days' time we enter the ship. It seals and we prepare for the journey home. We use these days to get settled in before takeoff. There is a time when we shall be in complete darkness as all the power in the ship is gathered in the thrust of leaving Earth's orbit. After that, it is just a long, but interesting, journey home. There is so much to do as we become our true selves."

"*Your* true selves," said Nesta sharply.

"And yours. You are our daughter. Whatever, whoever, we are, so too are you. You have to understand that."

"And what of Ormingat?" said Nesta. "What is it really like?"

"It is fair and just and good," said Matthew. "Of that I am quite, quite sure."

"But what does it look like, what does it feel like?"

said Nesta, pursuing the point her father knew she would, asking the question virtually impossible to answer.

"I don't know," said Matthew.

Nesta felt stunned at his words. What a terrible admission!

"I have a human brain with human knowledge," Matthew went on. "A vision of Ormingat is outside my range."

Nesta turned angrily to her mother.

"What about the doors," she said, "and the walls that glowed?"

"That was a story for a child, Nesta," said her mother. "I never pretended to you that it was true."

"And the twin suns, and the figure-of-eight orbit?" said Nesta, remembering the story as well as she remembered "The Little Mermaid" or "Aladdin and His Lamp," better perhaps because she had heard it more often.

"I made them up," said her mother. "At least, I think I did. I am never quite sure. We might get back there and discover it was true after all."

This was beyond Nesta's understanding.

"You said you were born there, grew up there, married there," she said. "If that is true, you must remember it."

She turned to her father for an explanation.

"I have no recollection at all of Ormingat," he said.

"Perhaps there is a silver stream meandering down a pale-blue hill, but I tend to imagine things. I know only that it is a good place and often I ache to see it again, to be there and to be part of it."

"But *why* do you not remember?" Nesta insisted.

"Let me just try to explain," said Matthew. "To human beings, the human brain seems infinite. It is not. The best memory in the world sometimes has to lose something to acquire new knowledge. So when we were endowed with human bodies for our time on Earth, you just cannot ignore the fact that we also had to have human brains. In them is embedded the knowledge of our fictional early lives in Boston. This is not simply a clever cover story. In a sense, we *were* there and the story is true."

"But no one in Boston will be able to remember you," Nesta objected. "Not if you weren't *really* there."

Matthew smiled wryly.

"Well, we shall certainly never go to America—that might stretch the illusion too far. But if someone from Boston walks into the bank—it has happened, a few times—he or she will promptly be made to recall knowing me at Boston Latin or meeting me at the University Club or some such. What is more, I shall share the memory and know exactly what to say. I believe I even worked a spell at State Street Bank—except I couldn't have, no matter what this brain of mine might tell me."

Nesta's face was the picture of bewilderment. Matthew clasped her hand and said softly, by way of explanation, "That is the power of Ormingat: the power to create an illusion. It is a very, very small branch of Ormingatrig knowledge, the same knowledge that makes diminution possible, that makes traveling faster than the speed of light irrelevant. It is all part and parcel of our science."

"And that is why you cannot remember the place you were really born?"

"That's it. Our human brains are taken up with human knowledge. It is only without our deeper selves that intuition preserves a memory of the goodness and the love we know is there, waiting to welcome us home."

Nesta suddenly felt exhausted.

Alison was quick to see her daughter's tiredness, much quicker than Matthew.

"Nesta needs time to get used to all these new ideas," she said. "We'll have tea now and talk again later. That seems sensible to me. What do you think?"

"Yes," said Matthew. "You're right. Tea, Nesta?"

Nesta nodded but said no more. She had made her declaration; and she knew in her heart of hearts that nothing would make her change her mind.

Do *they* love me enough to change theirs?

"What happens if you don't go?" she said.

"If we are not on the ship when the countdown is

completed, it will shoot off into space without us. Our contact with home will be broken forever."

"Would they punish you?"

Matthew smiled wistfully.

"To lose all possibility of returning to Ormingat would be punishment enough. I do not wish to grow old and die on this sad Earth."

Nesta sat back, silenced.

# CHAPTER 17

# Forewarned Is Forearmed

Monday teatime, Stella was walking through her front gate with a bag full of groceries when she saw Rupert again. She knew he was on the prowl—that much anyone could have guessed—but she also had a very good idea where he would be going.

"If someone comes asking questions about Thomas," she had said to Mickey when they had passed each other in the street on Saturday, "don't tell him anything you believe to be a secret. Some things are best kept to yourself."

So when Mickey got home and found his mother giving tea and biscuits to the stranger, he knew what to expect. He frowned at his mother.

"This is Mr. Shawcross," said Mrs. Trent quickly. "He is one of the people who are looking for Thomas

Derwent. He thinks someone may have taken him away against his will."

"Not quite that," said Rupert, steering clear of telling a palpable lie. "We simply do not know how he went, whether willingly or not. There are a number of possibilities. But the more information we can get hold of, the better chance we have of finding him."

He turned very abruptly toward Mickey.

"When was the last time *you* saw him?"

"Before Christmas," said Mickey's mother, not giving her son the chance to answer. "Like I told you."

"Well?" said Rupert, still looking at Mickey.

"Before Christmas, when he was in the hospital. We tried to get him to come home."

Rupert did not ask whom the *we* included. He did not need to. He went straight to the point.

"Why did he not come?" he said in a friendly voice. An honest answer to this question would have been very illuminating. Mickey gave an answer that was less than honest. He felt entitled to. People who ask impertinent questions have no right to be told the truth.

"I don't know," he said. "The hospital wouldn't let him go."

The true answer came unbidden to his mind: Thomas had refused to be taken back to Belthorp. He had been determined to wait for his father to collect him and take him away in *a spaceship the size and shape*

111

*of a golf ball.* Mickey's natural honesty made even a half-truth difficult.

Mickey's mother saw the embarrassment in her son's face and said quickly, "I know you have your job to do, Mr. Shawcross, but I cannot have my son upset. We like to help, where we can. But Mickey has told you all he knows. That will have to be enough."

"Just one more question, Mrs. Trent, if you don't mind," said Rupert. "Then I shall be going to catch my train. It isn't much."

Mrs. Trent nodded. If the man was going to catch his train, they would soon be rid of him. She had not wanted to invite him in at first, but he was polite and official. Jenny Trent was basically shy. She did not know how to be rude to people.

"One final question then," said Rupert, taking out his notebook and Biro. "Now, Mickey, I want you to think very carefully before you answer. Did Thomas at any time say anything that sounded to you strange or weird? Was there ever anything said about his name or the name of the place he came from?"

"Yes," said Mickey, brightening.

"What did he say?" said Rupert, eagerly sucking the point of the pen to make sure the ink would run freely.

"It wasn't what *he* said," said Mickey. "It all started with Miss Crosbie at school. She said because my second name was Trent and Thomas was called Derwent, we were like two rivers: the Trent and the Derwent are both tributaries of the River Ouse. That's how we first became friends."

The story was true, but it had nothing whatsoever to do with aliens or spaceships or any other extraterrestrial paraphernalia.

Rupert sighed. It was certainly not what he had been hoping to hear.

"But Thomas, Thomas himself, did he never tell you anything—anything secret?"

Mickey looked annoyed. His mother caught his glance and decided it was time to send their visitor on his way. Not easy, but clearly necessary.

"You said one more question, Mr. Shawcross," she said. "That would be two. Besides, you won't want to miss your train. It's a ten-minute walk from here to the station."

She stood up and went out into the passage, calling back over her shoulder, "I'll just get your coat for you."

Rupert followed her reluctantly, put on his coat, and was maneuvered to the door. Even after the door was opened and he was out on the doorstep, he tried to go on talking. Mrs. Trent would have none of that.

"I'm sorry, Mr. Shawcross, but I really have to shut the door. This house is drafty enough without letting more cold air in. My son catches cold so easily."

On Tuesday morning, on his way to school, Mickey met Mrs. Dalrymple. She had been deliberately looking for him.

"Well," she said, "what did you think of Mr. Shaw-cross?"

"He was nosy," said Mickey.

"Did you tell him anything?"

"I told him about Thomas and me being two rivers, but he wasn't interested. I thought he was going to write it down, but he didn't bother."

Stella laughed.

"Well, you had to tell him *something*, didn't you?"

Mickey smiled. He liked Mrs. Dalrymple. Never had he fully acknowledged to her what he now believed about Thomas and his father. But then, she had never broached the subject with him. Each knew what the other believed but thought it was best left unsaid.

As he walked away, however, Mickey did say, "I'm glad you warned me about him. I thought very hard about what I was going to say. I was ready for him."

# CHAPTER 18

# Nesta's Decision

At morning break Nesta and Amy sat together on a bench in the cloakroom. It was a cold, damp day and the rules about going out were fortunately relaxed. Mrs. Powell insisted on orderly behavior; prefects and duty staff made themselves visible, but she could see no point in driving hard bargains. So, on days like this, classrooms and corridors and cloakrooms were all available. Nesta and Amy had the junior cloakroom virtually to themselves, a good place for a quiet conversation.

"Listen, Amy," said Nesta as soon as they were settled. "I have something to tell you."

Amy looked at Nesta's intense expression and knew that the *something* must be serious.

"And you mustn't tell anybody else," Nesta went on,

"even if you think telling might help. It wouldn't. It's not like the time I was being bullied. You'll have to promise not to tell a soul."

"If you don't trust me, don't tell me," said Amy, not huffily but in her usual commonsense manner. "I never break promises. So if I promise not to tell, I won't, no matter what."

"Well, promise, then. Solemnly promise," said Nesta. Her eyes darkened. She gripped Amy's arm.

Amy smiled slightly and pushed her glasses back onto the bridge of her nose. "I, Amy Brown, do solemnly swear never to tell anybody whatever you trust me with now."

"Don't make fun, Amy. I mean it."

"So do I," said Amy. "It might have sounded like fun, but I mean every word. So what is the secret?"

"I'm going to run away," said Nesta simply, and then waited for what Amy would say to that.

Amy was startled. She looked hard at Nesta but said nothing. She had made a promise, and already she felt like breaking it! Running away was dangerous. Nesta could have no idea what she was thinking about.

"I've made up my mind," Nesta said. "I am running away from home and I won't come back till Sunday."

That was puzzling, but it made a difference. A time limit on running away from home made it not so drastic somehow. A promise *is* a promise.

"I think I might understand better if you told me

why," said Amy. "Is it to do with your parents moving back to Boston?"

"Sort of," said Nesta. "I can't tell you everything properly; but I hope I can tell you enough. Early on Thursday morning we are meant to be traveling to London. We'll stay there till Saturday, and on Saturday night we are supposed to be flying to America. Only *I* won't be with them because I am not going."

Amy gave a sigh of exasperation.

"What good do you think running away will do? They'll only wait till you come back, and then they'll still go. So all you'll be doing is postponing it. There's no point."

"That's the bit I can't tell you," said Nesta. "You'll just have to take my word for it. If they don't go this week, they won't be going at all."

"Are you sure?" said Amy doubtfully. "I mean, it does seem an odd way of doing things."

"There are reasons, reasons I can't tell you about. But I am absolutely sure. There is just one danger— the possibility that they might decide to go without me."

"Parents don't do that," said Amy. "I'm sorry to say it, Nesta, but you're talking complete rubbish."

"That's what I really hope," said Nesta. "It is what I am relying on. I disappear; they don't go; and their chance of going is lost."

"They'll call the police as soon as they know you're

missing," said Amy. "I wish I could get you to be more practical!"

"That's where I need your help and advice. Where can I spend four nights in the middle of winter without being found? After Saturday's over, I *want* to be found. I'll go back of my own accord. It isn't really proper running away. It's going into hiding."

"Why don't you just ask me the winning numbers for next week's lottery?" said Amy. "I've no idea where you can . . ."

Her voice tapered off as the thought came to her.

And at that moment, the bell rang for the end of break.

"I'll have to dash," said Amy. "If I'm late for Miss Edwards's lesson, she'll tear me to shreds. We'll talk about it at lunchtime. I do have an idea. I don't know whether you'll like it."

"Beggars can't be choosers," said Nesta. "I just knew you would help!"

They separated—Amy to needlework, Nesta to art.

At lunchtime they met in the sandwich room, where those who chose not to eat a school lunch were allowed to take their own food.

"All right, then," said Nesta as soon as they met, "what is this idea of yours? I could hardly work last lesson for wondering about it."

"It's simple," said Amy. "You can stay in our garage. For three nights anyway. Saturday wouldn't be safe because my brother comes home from college at the weekend and he keeps his bike in there. The garage is never used for anything else in the winter, except storage. We haven't got a car. Neither my dad nor my mum can drive. That might sound strange to you, but it does happen!"

It had the makings of an attractive idea, but Nesta could see snags. How would she get in and out? Where would she sleep? Go to the loo? Get food and drink? Amy was supposed to be practical. Surely she knew all these basic faults in the plan?

"I know what you're thinking," said Amy, "but your house is not the same as ours. Yours is a twentieth-century semi with the garage at the front attached to the house. Our street is Victorian. The garage is a later addition, completely separate from the house, built in the backyard with double doors leading onto the lane. There's a side door out to the yard, and an ordinary yard door to go out into the lane. There's even a toilet in there. Dad calls it the 'thunderbox.'"

That sounded better, but some basic questions had not been answered.

"Your family would twig," said Nesta. "Even if you could sneak me in somehow, I'd need to see you. You would be my contact with the outside. And your parents are bound to wonder if you start going into the garage at odd times."

"And that's another thing," said Amy. "I get home an hour before everyone else. Till this year, I had to go next door to Mrs. Tully's; but she moved away, and my parents decided that since I was nearly thirteen they would give me a key to let myself in."

"It's workable!" said Nesta, suddenly excited at really being able to do what she had blindly decided must be done before she had even considered how. "All I have to do is leave very early on Saturday morning before anyone's up. Then there'll only be one day and one night to go. You're a genius, Amy Brown! Has anybody ever told you that?"

"Frequently," said Amy. "But do calm down. There are still all sorts of complications. Just because it's 'workable' doesn't mean it's going to be easy."

Nesta became thoughtful.

"And I know what I can do on Saturday," she said. "I'll take a train journey. I'll get the train to Casselton and spend the night there."

"Why Casselton?" said Amy. "It's miles away."

"Why not Casselton?" said Nesta. "It's a big town. Big towns feel safer, so long as you stick to the main streets and don't go down back alleys. I've heard there's a supermarket there that's open all night!"

"You'll need money," said Amy. "Train tickets aren't cheap."

"I have money," said Nesta. "There's twenty-two pounds in my box, left over from Christmas, and I've got over fifty pounds in my savings bank that I can draw out if I need it. I went alone and took some out before Christmas to buy presents and nobody objected."

After school Amy walked with Nesta to the bus stop. Amy's face, always cheerful, was animated with intrigue. Her cheeks were red apples and her dark, frizzy hair looked like live wire.

"I have been thinking about it," she said. "I'll get things ready for you, make you a really safe cubbyhole. There's not much in there except boxes left over from the Christmas presents. I'll sneak some scatter cushions in from my bedroom and anything else I might think of. You'll come straight home with me after school tomorrow and I'll get you settled in before anyone else arrives. It could be fun!"

"I've been thinking too," said Nesta, looking less than happy now. "I don't want to get you into trouble. I shouldn't have asked you to help. It wasn't fair."

"Of course you should ask me to help. I'm your friend and I want to help. And it is only for a few days, you know. It's not proper running away. This time next week it will all be over."

What a wonderful, blissful thought!

The bus was in sight at the corner of the street.

Other children were milling forward, ready to push their way onto it. Amy was about to turn and leave Nesta to join the throng, but she stopped to say, "Besides, I made you a promise. If I want to keep it, I have to make sure you're safe!"

# CHAPTER 19

# Tuesday at Home

"What will happen to Charlie?"

Nesta was back home, sitting on the sofa, the cat straddling her knee again. The question was academic, so sure was Nesta that she would not be leaving. But to talk was easier than to be silent.

Matthew had not arrived yet. Alison, from her armchair, where she sat curled up drinking tea and warming her hands against the cup as on any other cold day, said, "You don't need to worry about that. I know you'll miss her at first, but that can't be helped. We are not permitted to take living creatures back to our own planet. Charlie will find someone else to love, honey. Cats are like that."

Her words filled Nesta with anger. This "not permitted" business made Ormingat sound even worse, if that were possible. But what she actually said to her mother was, again, academic. The anger stayed hidden.

"How do you know?" she asked. "How do you know that she won't become a stray, rummaging among rubbish for her food?"

"I know," said Alison. "I just know. Try to imagine that this house is a set on a stage and we are taking part in a play. The characters are real for the time the play lasts. The set is real. The cat is real. Then, when it is all over, the actors become themselves again and the stagehands clear everything away. Ormingat can manage to do that in ways that no one on Earth can ever envisage. Charlie, somehow, and I know not how, will be taken care of and will continue to have all the love and comfort she has had with us."

"You really believe that, don't you?" said Nesta, trying hard to grasp what was being said. "That's some faith!"

"It's not," said her mother gently. "It is absolute certainty."

Nesta felt the hairs prickle on the back of her neck. *I am not a child,* she thought, *not anymore. And I don't have to go along with everything you say.* Naturally, these were thoughts she kept to herself.

"I'd like to read those newspapers again," she said

quite smoothly. "Knowing more about the boy who disappeared from Casselton General might help me."

"*You're* not thinking of disappearing?" said her mother with a smile as she took the newspapers from the sideboard. It was banter and taken as such. The last thing Nesta needed was to arouse suspicion.

"I wouldn't know where to start," she said. "I don't have a magical, mystical spaceship!"

"Please understand, Nesta," said her mother more seriously, "the spaceship is neither magical nor mystical. It is just a wonderful piece of Ormingatrig technology."

When Matthew came home late from the bank, he seemed subdued. For the first time during the whole business, a feeling other than excited anticipation was gripping him.

"It'll be strange," he said. "After all these years, to be leaving everything behind. It feels almost like coming offstage after the play is over."

Nesta shuddered.

"How odd!" said Alison. "That's the metaphor I have just used!"

"It's true really," said Matthew. "We stop playing these parts and go back to being our real selves."

Nesta got up and scattered the newspapers and

the sleeping cat from her knee. This was just too much.

"I am my real self already," she snapped. "Do you not realize that?"

Matthew put one arm round her shoulders. "There's a level of real self you haven't reached yet," he said. "Just wait and see."

"I'm going to my room," said Nesta. "I don't want to talk about it anymore. I need a rest."

"After you've rested, you can pack the yellow bag with anything you want to take with you," said Matthew, giving her a comforting hug. "It's really going to happen, you know. And you *will* be happy!"

Nesta glared at him. *What will they do, then,* she thought, *inject me with happiness? Put me on a course of happy pills?* She grabbed Percy, the pajama case, and flounced out of the room with him. She did not slam the door. That would have been too clear an indication of how she felt.

Alison watched her go and bit her lip. It was going badly. She knew it was.

Matthew smiled hopefully.

"Looks as if she's getting more used to the idea," he said. "Percy must be going in the packing!"

Alison did not bother to argue. She just changed the subject.

"How was it at the bank? Did you give them any idea you might not be back?" she said.

"No," said Matthew as he warmed his hands at the fire. "I did my normal day's work. What happens next is not my worry."

In her room Nesta emptied all of the books out of her schoolbag and put back only those she would definitely need next day.

A voice from downstairs called up, "Remember, you don't need to go to school tomorrow unless you really want to."

Nesta went to her door and called down, "I really want to, Dad. I told you that already. I haven't changed my mind."

Then she went back to her packing.

Into the schoolbag she put a clean blouse, some clean underwear, and a box of tissues. Then she added the packet of half-chocolate biscuits she had smuggled from the cupboard in the kitchen. She got her bankbook from the drawer and her cash from the box she kept it in. These she placed carefully in the inner pouch of the schoolbag. By the time she had finished, there was just space left for her lunchbox, though she meant to buy a school lunch and save the sandwiches and fruit for later.

Into the yellow bag went Percy, a good space filler; two bottles of perfume still in their gift boxes; a canister of hair spray and two hairbrushes; and, finally, the China pig that stood on her dressing table. She felt the weight, looked at the bulk, added a few odds and ends for good measure, and then pulled the zip round it. Now it was as ready as it ever would be for its journey into space, a journey that, Nesta knew for certain, would never happen.

# CHAPTER 20

# Amy's Garage

"Well, what do you think of it?"

This was the question Amy had been dying to ask all day. The lessons at school were an irksome interruption of the important thing in life that day. At every opportunity, Nesta and Amy had talked furtively about their plans for the evening: what they would buy on the way home; how they would separate first, as if they were going different ways. Eventually, they met up again outside the Museum Gardens, as arranged. Then they took a short bus ride to Amy's house on Carthorpe Road. They hurried in the front door and straight out the back to a pleasant yard full of potted plants, with ramblers covering the high walls. With a flourish, Amy had opened the door that led from the yard into the garage. This was the hiding place!

She looked hopefully at Nesta as the two of them stood in the doorway, waiting for her approval. What was left of daylight came in from the very top of a side window where a bench was piled high with cardboard boxes so that no one passing the yard could see inside. This was the packaging left over from Christmas: Lego, Scalextrix, and a very big box that had contained some sort of karaoke machine. At the other side of the garage, in semidarkness, was a large workbench with a lathe fastened to one end of it and an old toolbox on the floor beneath. Other things were stored there: paint tins, a stepladder, an old metal clotheshorse, and several rusty buckets, some shrouded in dry cement. In the far corner, to the side of the big doors that led out onto the back lane, was a cubicle that clearly must be home to the "thunderbox."

"There's a light above the workbench," said Amy. "We can put it on now for a little while, till you're settled in, but it will have to be off before the others come home—it shines out into the yard when it is dark. I've brought you a bicycle lamp, and if we spread this old groundsheet over the clotheshorse, you can sit inside on my cushions and put it on quite safely. Don't have it on all the time, though, or the battery might go dead. Keep it for when you really need it."

"You've thought of everything," said Nesta.

The two of them rigged up the groundsheet tent and sat on the cushions to unpack the other things they had brought with them.

"Leave your food in your bag," said Amy. "Safest there—from dust, or anything else that comes looking, if you see what I mean."

"Mice?" said Nesta, horrified.

"Shouldn't think so," said Amy airily. "But there'll probably be a few spiders and moths and things like that."

Nesta swallowed but said nothing. She put her bottle of lemonade and the glass she had remembered to bring in one corner of the "tent." The cushions were very big floor cushions, well padded and comfortable. The bicycle lamp was placed on a small wooden box, very old and gnarled, that Amy had taken from under the workbench.

"You'll be quite snug in there," said Amy. It was almost a game. Amy half-wished that she could stay there herself!

Next, she showed Nesta the lavatory. It was very old with a high cistern and a huge pull chain. The walls were rough stone but painted white and very clean. The wooden lid to the toilet had clearly been kept well scrubbed. There was even a coconut mat on the floor. There was no window, of course, and no light.

"It's hardly ever used," said Amy, "but Mum says

that's no excuse for it to be dirty. So she gets rid of the cobwebs every month or so. It's just been done, as part of her new year cleaning. So she won't be coming in here for quite a while."

Amy took hold of the wooden handle at the end of the pull chain and pulled it downward like a bell rope. The cistern emptied with the force of a high waterfall, gave a great final gulp, and then began refilling like a thirsty giant glugging and slurping with no manners at all.

"The thunderbox!" said both girls together, and then giggled.

"Now," said Amy, "you must remember not to pull the chain till after eight-thirty in the morning. Anyone in our kitchen would hear it. The only safe time to pull it would be when you know that we are all out."

From an old chair to one side of the workbench, Amy now brought a very big overcoat.

"I don't know how cold it will get in here overnight. But this is Grandpa Turpin's old army greatcoat. It was the thickest thing I could find. If your own coat doesn't feel thick enough, put it round your shoulders. It's perfectly dry—I just brought it down here yesterday teatime."

"What will your grandpa say? Will he not miss it?" said Nesta.

Amy grinned.

"I don't think so, somehow," she said. "He's been dead for three years. He was a nice old man. He'd be pleased for you to have it."

The trouble with practical people is that they sometimes do not know what is going on inside other people's minds. . . .

"Now we'd better put the light out," Amy said. "And I'll have to go indoors and make myself a cup of tea like I always do. Better if you don't come in now—we've spent too much time out here for it to be safe. You've got your thermos flask? Keep the hot drink for later. I'll see you tomorrow teatime. I won't manage to come out before then. It would be too risky."

Nesta went with her to the door of the garage. In the darkness Amy looked up into the face of her friend and said something she'd been wondering about all day but felt shy of asking.

"I've been thinking," she said. "Your parents didn't tell the school you were leaving—and you told me it had to be a secret. They aren't running away from the law, are they? I mean, you've got to think, it's a funny way to go on."

Nesta almost laughed.

"No," she said. "Mom and Dad are far too honest and respectable for that! And I would love to tell you the truth, but there's no way you'd believe me even if I did."

Amy was relieved that Nesta had answered her question without annoyance, even though the answer was really no answer at all.

"Good night," she said. "See you tomorrow."

Alone in the darkness, Nesta quickly put the greatcoat on the workbench. She could not say it to Amy—it might seem ungrateful and hurtful—but she could not fancy using an old coat that belonged to a dead man.

She went into the tent, turned on the bicycle lamp, ate a sandwich from her lunchbox, and had a drink of lemonade. Then she put out the light, curled herself up on the cushions, and lay listening to the cassette player she had thankfully thought to bring. *I'll keep it on all night,* she thought. *The headphones will stop creepy-crawlies from getting into my ears!*

She looked at her watch over and over again. The pointers moved slowly from half past five, to six, and then to seven. Feeling colder, she hugged one of the big cushions for warmth and managed to drift off to sleep.

She woke with a start, feeling absolutely freezing and not quite sure where she was. The headphones were still on her ears, but the tape had run out, leaving her almost deaf. She groped about in the darkness, found the bicycle lamp, and managed to switch it on. It was still only ten to eight; the night had barely begun.

Then something moved. Out of the corner of her eye, she was aware of lethargic movement. She turned her head swiftly.

There on the cushion, just inches from her elbow, stretching its legs, was the biggest spider she had ever seen!

With an effort, she stopped herself from screaming, stood up quickly, and in so doing tipped over the makeshift tent so that the clotheshorse clattered to the ground. She felt paralyzed. *What to do, what to do, what to do . . .*

She held on to the lamp and shined it all round her feet, but the spider was gone. Fear can only last so long if you don't faint. She didn't faint, and so she began looking for a way out of this scary situation. She picked up one of the cushions, the one furthest away from where the spider had been, and shook it. Then (beggars certainly can't be choosers!), she grabbed the greatcoat from the workbench and went with it into the lavatory. The cushion she placed on the wooden seat, and the greatcoat she slung round her shoulders. Once the door was shut, she double-checked everything, and then switched off the bicycle lamp. Again she dozed off, her chin rubbing against the rough wool of the greatcoat's lapels.

The next time she woke up, not half an hour later, she was warmer inside the greatcoat. Quickly she switched on the bicycle lamp and could see that all was safe. This awakening should have been less terrifying; but as she looked down at the wide lapels of the greatcoat, she began to think of the old man who had been dead three years. Perhaps his spirit was there in the coat haunting her. She began to cry, quietly and miserably. She did not want to take the coat off: it would be so cold without it. But she became more and more afraid of keeping it on. The lapels moved up and down with her breathing. She watched them and wondered if it was her own breath or the breath of the dead man.

Then, suddenly, it was just as if a quiet voice spoke to her, the soft voice of an old, old man. *The dead cannot hurt you, love,* it whispered, *and if they could, do you think they would want to? Go to sleep now. That will make morning come faster.*

Nesta felt comforted and stopped crying. She pulled the collar of the coat up about her ears. She leant her head against the wall and, half-sitting, half-lying, she went into a sound sleep and did not wake till morning.

# CHAPTER 21

# Where Can She Be and What Can We Do?

When Nesta failed to return on the first bus, Alison decided to meet the next one. The bus stop was on the corner of the street, on the main road that led through the estate. It was visible from the front gate, but the darkness and a certain unspecified anxiety made Alison tense. She wanted to see her daughter step down from the next bus; yet she was visited by an overwhelming certainty that Nesta would not be on it.

The bus was five minutes late. It stopped and an old man Alison knew only by sight climbed up the steps slowly, clutching his walking stick. No one alighted. There were no passengers at all coming to Linden Drive. The next bus would be in half an hour's time. Alison stood dismayed. There was no point in standing in the cold for half an hour. Her own front door was hardly five minutes away.

"What if she's run away?" said Alison to Matthew after she told him that Nesta had been on neither of the two buses she normally used. "She's never as late as this without telling us."

"Check her room," said Matthew. "See if there's any sign there. But you know, for practical purposes, this is her last day on Earth. Maybe she's stopped to talk to friends, or to look at places she has cared about here. There are all sorts of explanations."

In Nesta's room there was no note on the dressing table; nothing appeared to be missing that might not be stuffed in the yellow bag that was on the floor at the foot of her bed, apparently all packed and ready to go.

"We should check the bag," said Alison.

"She was told she could take whatever she wanted. I don't like prying," said Matthew.

Alison looked at him, exasperated.

"Ideals are all very well, but Nesta is very late and we have the right and the duty to find out all we can, even if it means opening her bag. You're a hard man to understand, Matthew Gwynn!"

"Open it then," said Matthew softly. "Open it, *Athelerane.*"

Alison blushed at his use of her true name in a tone that made it sound like an endearment. Anxiously, she pulled the zip round the end of the yellow bag; its lid flopped back and an envelope fell to the floor. Her heart was filled with dread as she picked it up.

"To Mom and Dad" was the inscription. The flap was sealed down and Alison tore it open. She trembled as she removed the letter from inside. She hesitated, then handed it to Matthew.

"You read it," she said. "I can't."

Matthew read in silence.

*Dearest Mom and Dad,*

*You told me so much, but you would not listen to what I had to say. I am not coming to Ormingat. I am never coming to Ormingat. I am Earthborn and Earthbound. I do love you very much. If you leave without me, I do not know what I shall do. If you stay, I promise to come home when the danger is past. In the meantime, don't worry. I shall take great care to run no risks.*

*From your loving daughter,*
*Nesta*

"What does she say?" said Alison.

"She will not be home till Sunday," said Matthew. "By which time, we shall be gone; or we shall be here for good. She speaks of being 'Earthbound.' That is what we shall be if we fail to leave on Sunday morning. She cannot know what that really means to us. There was no way of explaining it to her properly."

Alison took the letter in her own hands and read it.

"She will take no risks!" she said. "No risks! She is too innocent. She has no idea what a risk is."

"Innocent she might be," said Matthew, "but she is not stupid. She'll do her best to stay out of danger."

"*You* are as innocent as she is," said Alison. "This is not Ormingat! There are evil people out there who are much cleverer than you imagine. Do you think wickedness is confined to avoidable back alleys? I'm phoning the police—now!"

Matthew was horrified.

"We can't show them that letter," he said. "It tells everything."

Alison paused with the receiver in her hand.

"We tell them that our daughter has failed to return home," she said, "nothing more."

"What time is it now?" said Matthew, being the practical one for once.

"Five to six."

"Nesta is nearly thirteen," said Matthew. "Children her age go missing for hours. The police would take no notice. It's not even especially late. They'll tell us to check her friends. They'll ask us if there is any special reason why we think she is genuinely missing. We'll draw attention to ourselves to no purpose whatever."

"Try the spaceship, then," said Alison. "We are expected there tonight. Go inside and ask the communicator to find her."

"There are many reasons why that is impossible," said Matthew. "Our language can act as a homing device, but homing devices work only if the holder of the key uses it and wants to be found. Nesta has disappeared of her own accord. Besides, she holds no key: she cannot say the words properly. But there is a more important reason. If I enter the spaceship tonight, I feel sure it will not allow me to leave."

"So what do we do?" said Alison.

"Tonight," he said, "all we can do is look for her ourselves."

"Where?" said Alison. "She could be anywhere in York. She could be on a bus or a train going out of York. She could be miles away."

"Or she could be with her friend. She could be somewhere with Amy Brown."

Alison looked at her husband with a glimmer of hope, but the hope was dashed straightaway as she realized that she did not know Amy's address. The friendly visits had not had time to get off the ground. Amy had been once to tea at Linden Drive. Nesta had not yet returned Amy's visit. It had never seemed necessary to know where Amy lived.

They searched Nesta's room, this time hoping to find the address written down somewhere. It was then they found that her moneybox was empty.

"She had over twenty pounds in there," said Alison.

They emptied the yellow bag and discovered that it

was stuffed with things that were mostly there as deceptive bulk.

"Her bankbook isn't anywhere either," said Alison. "She must have taken that. So we can guess she has money with her. I don't know whether that is better or worse."

"The telephone directory," suggested Matthew. "We might find Amy's address from that."

"With a name like Brown?" said Alison. "There could be hundreds of them. They might not even be in the book. We aren't!"

Matthew sighed.

"Tomorrow we can ask the school," he said. "They will have her address."

Alison was aghast.

"If she is not home by tomorrow morning, very early tomorrow morning," she said, "I shall definitely ring the police. They will not ignore a child being missing overnight."

The horror of Nesta being missing overnight was too chilling to contemplate. Here was a woman of Ormingat suddenly confronted with the possibility of sharing in the agony of Earth. This was something that happened to other people, something that happened only to Earthlings.

Alison laid her head on her arms and wept.

Matthew did not know what to do.

"You wait here by the phone in case she rings," he said. "I'll go and look for her."

He took the car out and drove round York, up one street, down another, hoping against hope to catch sight of his daughter. Once he even drove past the end of Carthorpe Road where Nesta, wrapped in Grandpa Turpin's greatcoat, was already fast asleep. After three hours of fruitless searching, he turned for home.

Alison was still awake and waiting when he came in, her face chalk white, her eyes red with weeping.

# CHAPTER 22

# Amy on Thursday

All day Thursday, Amy waited for a summons that never came.

She had worked it out that Nesta's parents would report her missing to the police. Then a police officer would come to the school to make inquiries. He or she would want to question Nesta's best friend. That seemed logical. Amy Brown was no fool.

*I'll just say I don't know. There is no getting past "I don't know," so long as I look surprised and worried. It won't be hard to look worried!*

When Mrs. Powell came into the French lesson, Amy tried hard to hear what she was saying to Miss Simpson, but their voices were low and they were evidently discussing some piece of school business. As the headmistress left the room, she did not even look at

Nesta's empty seat and did not give a glance in Amy's direction.

By lunchtime Amy had come round to thinking that maybe the police had got her address and gone straight round there to ask her parents, *who will not be at home.* Each day, Amy's father went off to work first. Then her mother took Gerard, her younger brother, to the junior school where his grandmother would pick him up at teatime. He would stay at Granny's house till Mrs. Brown returned from work. That was why Amy was always first home.

*If the police can't get an answer, they'll come back to the school.*

Yet home time came and still nothing had happened. Nobody asked her why Nesta was absent. No one assumed that she would know anything. She did not know whether to feel relieved or alarmed. On the bus home she was so deep in thought trying to work out all the possibilities that she almost passed her own stop.

She hurried down her street, practically ran through the front gate and up the steps, shot through the house, and was all fingers and thumbs opening the back door. When she got into the garage, she found Nesta sitting on the stool, her arms folded on the bench, and her head resting on the greatcoat as she dozed.

"I'm back," said Amy. "How's it been?"

Nesta sat up, startled.

"It's been a long day," she said, "and the night was even longer!"

"What have you done?" said Amy.

"Not a lot," said Nesta wearily. "I've eaten everything and drunk all the pop and all the tea in my flask. I've read the magazines and part of my library book. In between, I slept and I listened to my radio."

"Come inside for a while," said Amy, looking at her watch. "Bring the flask and the lunchbox. We'll have time to stock you up before anyone's due home. And I'll get a carrier bag for you to put the rubbish in the wheelie bin."

Nesta sat on the chair in Amy's kitchen, thankful to be in a warm house again under a cheerful light. Amy's kitchen was much bigger than the one at home, with a square table right in the middle of the floor and rugs covering the lino. Set in one wall was a three-bar electric fire that gave a cheerful warmth. In different circumstances, Nesta would have enjoyed getting to know this big old house. Today, she had too much on her mind.

"One thing about the radio," she said as soon as she sat down, "I kept it tuned to the local station, but there was nothing on about me being missing, nothing about any missing schoolgirl. I thought there might have been. Did anybody mention me at school?"

"No," said Amy. "You were just marked absent. Mrs. Purvis didn't even ask if I knew what was the matter with you. She was more concerned with the note Jack Patterson brought. He'd been off for three days with a gumboil!"

"My mom and dad mustn't have reported me missing," said Nesta, almost tearful. "Maybe they don't care where I am. Maybe they're already on the way to London."

"Of course they're not. Perhaps the police are just keeping it quiet for a day or so in case you turn up. I mean, if they kept it quiet till Sunday, you would turn up, wouldn't you?"

It was almost as if Amy had read the note that Nesta had left!

"You're clever," said Nesta with a watery smile. "Sometimes I think you're too clever by half!"

"I'm not clever enough to know what you mean by that!" said her friend as she filled the flask and started making fresh sandwiches. Amy was, as always, very well organized.

"Here," she said, handing Nesta a cup, "drink that, then rinse the cup and put it away. I'll have your rations ready in two ticks."

Ten minutes before her mother and brother were

due home, Amy went with Nesta to the garage to settle her in for the night.

"And here are four more batteries in case yours run dead. You wouldn't want to be without your music or your radio. And here's a big battery for the torch. It's a long-life—so I think it would last all right even if you kept it on all night."

"I'll pay you for them," said Nesta. She hesitated and then added, "I want to ask you another big favor."

"Ye-es," said Amy cautiously, wondering what was coming next.

"Could you do some shopping for me tomorrow? I'll give you the money."

"What is it you want?"

"Well," said Nesta, "I have had all day to think about it. If the police are looking for me, I should do every-thing I can to keep a low profile. Could you go to the station and get me a return ticket to Casselton on the earliest train on Saturday? Then if they inquire at the station with my description, I have more chance of not being found out. You don't look anything like me."

"I know!" said Amy, pulling a comical face. "They'll be looking for somebody tall, fair, and thin. And I'm fat, dark, and little."

"That's not what I mean," said Nesta. "You know it isn't. And you will go, won't you?"

"Well, it'll have to be in the lunch hour," said Amy,

148

studying the problem. "There wouldn't be time for me to go shopping after school and get back here before Mum and Gerry. But I'll do what I can."

"And there is one other thing," said Nesta. "I hate to ask you, but it could help."

"Ask," said Amy, "and be quick. We haven't much time."

"Get me a red fleece jacket from the store near your bus stop. I have never had a fleece jacket before, and I don't like the color red. So that'll be another way of disguising myself."

Nesta handed Amy her purse with the money she had drawn from the bank in it in addition to the notes she had brought from the box in her bedroom.

"What's in there should be more than enough," she said.

Five minutes to go.

"I can't stay any longer," said Amy. "I'll have to double-check indoors. Still, so far so good. One night over, two left to go. Though what you'll do after that worries me. Saturday night in Casselton?"

"It'll just be the one night," said Nesta. "And I'll be able to give myself up very early Sunday morning."

Amy shrugged. There was something unsatisfactory about the whole situation, but it was too late to do anything about it now. As Granny Turpin would say, in for a penny, in for a pound!

Alone in the garage again, Nesta was beginning to feel quite at home. She had her supplies, her deadline, and—this will sound strange to you—the company of a friendly greatcoat whose owner wished her well.

# CHAPTER 23

# Thursday at the Gwynns'

It was all very well Alison saying that she would ring the police first thing in the morning. But when it came to the point, lifting the phone to say "My daughter is missing" was much more difficult than she had anticipated.

"Nesta is not missing," Matthew pointed out. "She has not been abducted, she has not mysteriously vanished: she has run away. The police will want to know why. How will we explain it?"

Alison looked at him, hesitating, with the receiver already in her hand.

"What use will they be anyway?" said Matthew. "How often, I wonder, do they find youngsters who have deliberately run off?"

"They can find them dead," said Alison with a shudder.

Then, after a silence, she said, "If we report her missing, we shall at least have something to hold on to, some possibility."

So it went on. There was thought and counter-thought as the Gwynns struggled to know what to do for the best.

"I don't know what we should do," said Matthew at length. "We've talked round and round in circles. It isn't becoming any clearer to me. All I hope is that Nesta has found herself somewhere safe to stay and that, as she thinks about it, she'll realize that her place is here with us. She could walk in the door anytime. Then we would be off and away."

"Oh, Mattie!" said Alison. "You *know* she won't come back in time. She's made that quite clear. She wants us to stay here and this is her way of making sure that we do. And what happens next? After the ship goes, where does that leave us? Neither of Earth nor of Ormingat? What will we be?"

Alison was on the edge of a great and frightening thought. But no way would this make her consider the possibility of leaving her child behind.

"How does she know that we won't go without her?" said Matthew impatiently, far more aware than his wife of what they were being forced to give up. It was as if he really knew the edge and what was over it. "We could. We would have every right to. The stakes are high."

Alison gave him a look of disbelief.

"And what would happen to her? Left here on Earth alone?"

"She would be taken care of," said Matthew. "If they can take care of a house and a cat, taking care of a child should be no problem. They would create another illusion. We remember Boston, don't we?"

Alison shuddered.

"You do see what I mean, don't you?" said Matthew.

"At this moment, Mattie, I see nothing. My eyes are too full of tears. You talk as if Nesta were safe and sound. Other children have been raped and murdered. What makes you think that our child is immune?"

When dusk came again, Alison and Matthew stood together looking from the back window into the garden, across the patio and the lawn to the pond where the frog squatted on its gray stone lily pad.

"Ask the communicator," said Alison. "It is all we can do, and we must do something."

"I've already told you," said Matthew, "if I enter the spaceship, I will not be allowed to leave."

"We'll drain the pond," said Alison. "Then we'll lift the frog. We'll lift it just so far, and we'll call down for help without entering the spaceship at all."

"That would never work," said Matthew, but his tone

belied his words. Maybe it would work. Maybe it was worth a try.

"It's worth a try," said Alison, echoing his thought.

So together in the growing darkness they went to the pond, drained it, and then tugged at the frog till it tilted, leaving a gap between itself and the pad.

"Help us," called Matthew, bending low and cupping his hands to call downward into the deaf ear. "We have lost our daughter."

From the gap came a streak of blue light. Matthew and Alison felt it drawing them like a powerful magnet. As they struggled backward their clothes clung round them. Alison had to tear her skirt away from the opening that widened like jaws endeavoring to swallow them. Matthew flung himself at the frog and pushed it back into place. The power was muffled now but still strong, throbbing beneath the stone as if gathering more strength. Matthew grabbed Alison by the hand and ran with her into the house. As if on cue, large drops of rain began to spatter down on them. They locked the door behind them and went straight to the front room, out of sight and sound and, hopefully, influence of the communicator's will.

"It is only thinking of our own good," said Matthew, panting and wiping his brow with his handkerchief. Short as had been their time in the rainstorm, both had wet hair and shoulders soaked with rain.

"It is not thinking in that way at all," said Alison bitterly. "It is not a sentient being. It is an artifact, a thing, a programmed machine. I should have known better. What we have just done is like asking a phone for help with no one at the other end picking up the receiver."

"It was *your* idea," said Matthew. "Not mine."

"I know," said Alison wearily, "and I know now that I was wrong."

"So what do we do?" said Matthew.

"Bang our heads against the nearest brick wall," said Alison angrily.

"We can pray, *Athelerane*," said Matthew helplessly. "I don't really know what more we can do."

"Prayer is not something I have gone short on, *Maffaylie*. I won't sleep but I must lie down. I feel too weak to go on."

Her face was white against the darkness of her damp hair. Her eyes were circled with deep shadows.

At three in the morning the clock radio by their bed began to buzz again. Matthew and Alison were instantly alert. They gazed eagerly at the clock face, waiting for the voice that would surely tell them what to do.

"Return-to-the-ship," it said. "Your-return-is-awaited."

"But what of our daughter?" said Alison. "What of Nesta?"

"Return-to-the-ship," said the metallic voice. "It-is-time-to-return."

155

"I have lost my daughter," said Alison angrily, irritated by the automaton. "What can I do?"

"Return-to-the-ship," said the voice.

Matthew listened and knew that they must find some other way of asking the question. The machine might know the answer, if only they knew the right way to ask.

"Find our daughter," he said.

"On-Earth," said the machine, "use-Earth-means."

"Tell what Earth means are," said Matthew. He and Alison waited anxiously for the reply, which did not come immediately.

"Ask-Earth-authorities," said the voice at last, clearly experiencing some difficulty. Maybe the effort of communicating through this nonstandard contraption was just too great.

"Report her disappearance to the police here in York?" said Matthew.

The computer groaned, or maybe it was just the clock.

"Return-to-the-ship," it said. "Your-return-is-awaited."

Then the clock fell silent and became itself again.

"Not a lot of help," said Matthew.

"Enough to give us the next step," said Alison firmly. "We *do* ring the police. We tell them that Nesta has not come home. It is surely time we did."

"In the morning," said Matthew, "in daylight. We are

156

so confused now we would not know what we were saying."

Alison lay back on her pillow, but first she unplugged the clock from the wall socket. A futile gesture maybe, but she was beyond knowing what was futile and what was not. She was worried and miserable and very, very angry.

At first light Matthew crept out and turned the valve that filled the pond. It would not do to have policemen wondering why it was empty, or getting too close to the frog on the lily pad.

# CHAPTER 24

# Friday in Carthorpe Road

"I skipped games," said Amy when she came to the garage at teatime on Friday. "It was the last lesson of the day. They were just messing about in the gym because the field was too wet. Miss Garth is always flustered when that happens. No one will be any the wiser. It gave me more time to get all the shopping done."

She put down in front of Nesta three large bags—evidence of her spending spree. In one was a red fleece—*with a hood*! A second bag contained a thick white sweater, and in the third was a pair of black leggings and some knee-length boots.

"I got them as cheap as I could," said Amy. "The sweater came from the Oxfam shop. I just thought that if you are going to look different at all, you will have to look completely different. We can put your school things in the karaoke box for now."

"What if your brother looks inside it?"

"He won't. It's just a family habit to hang on to the boxes during the guarantee period in case anything has to be taken back to the shop. Just before next Christmas, Mum will have a clearance and they'll all be crushed up and put in the wheelie bin. We're a very methodical family!"

"Did you get the train ticket?" asked Nesta, worried in case there had not been enough money left to pay for it.

Amy looked aghast for a moment, just long enough to fool her friend. Then she said, "Look, Nesta, don't you know by now that I always do what I set out to do?"

From Nesta's purse she produced the ticket with a flourish. "One return to Casselton: seat booked for the journey there, journey home anytime within one month. I hope you are impressed."

She handed the purse back to Nesta.

"And I have spent less than half your money."

They left the bags on the garage floor and went indoors for a repeat of yesterday's effort. They drank Coke, made sandwiches, and then hurried to hide the evidence.

Nesta was just replacing a tea towel on the rack and

Amy was putting the glasses away in the cupboard; both girls suddenly froze. There was a noise from the front of the house. A door opened. Amy took one look at Nesta, then bustled her out the back door, closing it behind her. After one quick look round for anything they might have missed, she went out into the hall, calling, "We're running short of milk, Mum. Shall I go to the corner shop and get some?"

"No need, love," said her mother. "I went to Tesco's on the way home. I knew the milk was low."

Amy went forward and took her mother's shopping bags.

"You should be more help, Gerry," she said to her younger brother. "You're big enough to carry these."

"Don't start an argument," said Mrs. Brown. "I have not had the best of days. I could do with a little peace now I'm home!"

Nesta, meantime, had rushed down the back steps with such haste that, like a latter-day Cinderella, she lost a shoe. She dashed to retrieve it and, carrying it in her hand, she let herself into the garage and stood for several moments with her back to the door. Then, when her heart had stopped beating too fast, she went straight into the lavatory closet, not venturing to put anything away or try anything on till much, much later. She just sat on the cushioned seat, with the greatcoat wrapped round her, expecting to be hauled out of her hiding place and praying hard that she wouldn't be. As time passed she felt more secure. But still she did not move. She just sat in the dark going over her plans for the following day.

She would have to go through the yard and leave by the yard door to get into the lane: opening the big garage doors was out of the question. Then she would get to the bus stop on Maple Terrace and take the first bus that came, whether it was going to the station or not. She had time to fill in and a bus is warmer than a bus queue. She knew how to end up at the station in time and that was all that mattered.

Once at the station, she would get herself some breakfast at the Upper Crust. In her new clothes she would not look conspicuously young; she was sure she could pass for fifteen, or even sixteen. She was quite tall for her age, and the fleece with the thick jumper underneath would give her slight build a deceiving bulk. She was glad she had not bought a child's ticket for the train.

As the night drew on, however, she became less sanguine. It stuck in her like a dart that, so far as either she or Amy knew, her parents were making no attempt to find her. At her instigation, Amy had rung her home number. As planned, when the phone was answered, Amy had said in as grown-up a voice as she could manage, "Is that not Gaby's Hairdressing? . . . I'm sorry, I must have got the wrong number."

It was Matthew who answered the phone, and he

had accepted Amy's words without any suspicion. He had seized the receiver so hopefully, and was deeply disappointed. "Just a wrong number," he said. "Somebody wanting that hair salon again."

"So," Amy had said as they were sitting in the kitchen, "at least we know that they haven't gone to London."

That was on Thursday.

Now it was Friday: just one night before the spaceship would take off. Nesta began to feel utterly forlorn. Her parents would surely hang on till the very last minute, hoping she would join them. But Nesta, alone in the darkness with only Grandpa Turpin's greatcoat for comfort, was not so sure now that they would choose to remain on Earth for good. She did have some idea, after all, of what she was hoping they would do. She even realized what a sacrifice they would be making. *Why should they do that for me when I would not do as much for them?*

She began to weep quietly into the collar of the greatcoat, making it damp with her tears. *I was once an ordinary person with a mom and dad, like lots of other people. Now I feel as if I belong to nobody.*

*You belong to yourself,* said the coat. *You make your own decisions.*

There was a momentary temptation to surrender—to return to Linden Drive and accept the journey into space. Then the horror of that outweighed her agony and loneliness. *I am of Earth,* she sobbed, *and I shall stay on Earth. If after Sunday I am left all alone in this world, I shall just have to brave it out.*

Then—hopes have to be pinned somewhere—Nesta began to pin all of hers on the visit to Casselton and Belthorp. There she would find people who knew a child from Ormingat and who might welcome another young person linked to that planet.

*But I am Earthborn. If those people knew about Ormingat and if they helped that boy to go, they should help me to stay.* There was Jamie, who offered help to Tonitheen, and Stella Dalrymple, who spoke so mysteriously of "starlight." They were in some nebulous region between those who knew the secret and those who could not even hope to guess. *I must not tell because to tell is wrong; I must not tell because I would not be believed.* Here, though, were people who might not need to be told. Here were people who might already know.

# CHAPTER 25

# Friday in Linden Drive

The Gwynns were up and dressed well before daybreak. Matthew hesitated, and then plugged in the clock radio again.

"Some use that is!" said Alison.

"We might still get help from home," he said sheepishly. "They are bound to know what a quandary we are in."

Alison shrugged. As far as she was concerned the argument was over.

"We'll ring the police, as agreed," she said flatly. "That at least is in our control."

"Well, let's think it out first," said Matthew, still hoping for some sort of last-minute reprieve. "Let's plan what we are going to say."

Loyalty to Ormingat made them both determined

to do nothing that would betray their mother planet. So, between them, they constructed as logical a story as they could manage. They went over it again and again. It was late morning before they finally called the police. A very calm voice asked their name and address and a few questions, and then promised that someone would be sent round within the next few hours to take further particulars. It was impossible to tell what the man behind the voice was thinking, but there seemed no sense of urgency.

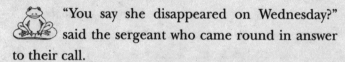 "You say she disappeared on Wednesday?" said the sergeant who came round in answer to their call.

"Yes," said Alison. "She went to school on Wednesday as usual and did not come home at teatime."

"But, Mrs. Gwynn," said the policeman, "it is now four-thirty on Friday. Why have you not called us before now?"

Alison opened her mouth to protest that they had reported Nesta's disappearance five hours ago, but Matthew held up his hand to silence her. Such a quibble could lead nowhere.

"We thought you wouldn't bother, and perhaps rightly so," he said hastily. "Nesta is not an infant. She is nearly thirteen. She took money with her and she left a note. We expected her to come back as soon as she realized how foolish she'd been."

"If I might see the note?" said the officer, still doubtful about the lateness of their report.

"I have it here," said Alison, handing him a folded paper.

He opened and read,

> Dear Mom and Dad,
>     I need to get away for a few days. I don't want to go to Boston. I want to stay here in York. This is where I was born. I'll come home soon. I want to give you time to think it over. I don't want to live anywhere else.
>
> Your loving daughter,<br>Nesta

"What does she mean about going to Boston?" said the sergeant.

"That is where we came from—before Nesta was born. We have been talking recently about the possibility of going back there," said Alison as smoothly as she could.

"She writes with a mature hand," said the sergeant, looking critically at Alison's forgery. The young constable with him sat silent, watching.

"She is bright for her age," said Matthew. "We think she will know what she is doing, but as the time goes on we are of course more anxious than at first. We thought she would have come home by now. Really, all we need to know is that no harm has come to her."

"We have had no reports of any incidents involving a young person fitting your daughter's description," said the policeman coldly. "We will naturally check with other forces in the area and do the usual hospital checks to make sure that she has not been admitted anywhere. We can also get her photograph into tomorrow's papers, with your consent."

He knew that there was something here that did not quite ring true. The woman looked distraught enough and her husband was clearly worried, but there was not that usual anxiety to shift the burden, to insist, however unrealistically, that the police should work flat out to find their daughter, abandoning all else.

"Do you mind if my colleague and I have a look round the house? It is normal procedure. We might see something you have missed."

*Like bloodstains on the carpet, or a body in the attic . . .*

"Now we'll just have a scout round the garden," said the sergeant after they had pounded up and down the stairs, finding nothing.

He caught the worried look Alison gave her husband and was intrigued.

"That won't be a problem, will it?" he said.

Alison shook her head mutely.

The two policemen went out of the front door into darkness. Their torches made pools of light as they went round the side of the house into the back garden. They inspected carefully the high hedge that separated the Gwynns from their neighbors, the Marwoods. Between the Gwynn house and Mrs. Jolly's there was a six-foot fence covered with a tangle of rambling rosebushes. At the bottom of the garden was the pond, and beyond that three tall old trees that predated the house. There were places to hide, but Nesta was not hidden there.

"Wow!" said the younger policeman as he shined his torch on the frog in the middle of the pond. "That's some piece of sculpture! It's big enough to stand outside the town hall! I wouldn't want it in my back garden."

On the grass beside the pond there was a large circle of flattened blades that looked as if something heavy and symmetrical had rested there recently. The older policeman looked down at it and shuddered. There was something wrong here and he did not know what it was. Part of him did not want to know, not if it meant that a child was dead.

They went back into the house.

"The grass near your pond has a flattened patch," said the sergeant, coming straight to the point. "Have you any idea what made it?"

"The roller," said Matthew quickly. "I had to turn it on its side when it got jammed. It's a hefty thing but it does make a good job of the lawn."

"In January?" said the sergeant, getting more and more worried.

"No," said Matthew with a nervous laugh, "of course not. That happened in September. I sprained my wrist turning it over and it was left there for a few days. I know it sounds a stupid thing to do. Every time I look at that stunted grass I wonder if it will ever come right again without replanting."

There was really no more the sergeant could say. After all, there was no evidence of digging or burial, just a fairy ring of flattened grass. Matthew looked sheepish enough to make the explanation sound true.

"Well," said the policeman, putting his notebook away in his pocket, "if you can give me a recent photograph of your daughter, we'll see it gets circulated. And what about the newspapers?"

"Yes," said Alison. "Put it in the paper—with the message that we want her to return home, and that we have changed our mind about leaving York. We wouldn't want to do anything that would make her so seriously unhappy."

The sergeant looked at her anxious face and felt reassured. It takes all sorts to make a world. If this pair appeared rather odd, perhaps it was to do with them being foreigners. They *were* foreigners. You could tell by the accent, though it wasn't very pronounced. And all that about going to Boston pointed to their being American. Americans, he believed, could be very cool customers!

"We'll keep you informed," he said. "And if your

daughter does turn up, you will naturally let us know straightaway."

"Of course," said Matthew. He showed them to the door and breathed a sigh of relief after it closed behind them.

"I'm glad he didn't ask to see the roller," he said.

"We haven't got one," said Alison. "There's only the lawn mower."

"Precisely," said Matthew, smiling weakly.

"If they ask about the roller again," he added, thinking rapidly, "I'll have to say I got rid of it because it was too heavy."

# CHAPTER 26

# Snow!

Early on Saturday morning Nesta looked out of the garage window into the yard. There was a light covering of snow illuminated by the lamplight shining in from the lane. Nesta shivered. Only a week ago she had sat with Amy in Sampson Square, on a day that seemed to promise an early spring. Now winter had returned, and just at the wrong time. *Still*, thought Nesta, *it could be worse; at least it has stopped snowing and that snow isn't deep.*

Methodically, she cleaned up, as much as possible, all trace of her having lodged there. Rubbish was put into plastic bags and placed in the Scalextrix box, ready for Amy to pick up at a later, safer time. Grandpa Turpin's greatcoat was carefully, and lovingly, folded and put into the karaoke box, the only box big enough to take it. Then Nesta put on the red fleece coat, pulling the hood over her head so that it hid her hair and most of her face. In the new clothes, she felt very different and hoped that this would mean that she looked different too. She double-checked everything: her purse, her ticket, loose change in her pocket, and the watch on her wrist that pointed to seven-forty-five. Already a gray dawn was beginning to creep. Nesta wished she had started her preparations sooner.

She opened the door into the yard. Holding her breath, she stepped out of the garage and looked up fearfully at the back bedroom windows, but the curtains were closed and there was no sign of life. As she turned away, a curtain twitched just too late for her to see it.

It was Amy. She had got up, and now she watched from above as her friend made good her retreat. She felt like tapping on the window to let Nesta know that she was not alone, but thought better of it. Seconds later, a bedroom door opened on the landing. Amy's heart was in her mouth! That would surely be her mother. Any minute now she might go downstairs into the kitchen. She would pull up the blinds and see a stranger in the backyard!

Amy said silently and urgently, *Hurry, Nesta, hurry!*

But Nesta was standing still, puzzling what to do.

Between her and the door that led to the lane was a stretch of concrete covered in a powdering of snow. So she had the problem of covering her tracks in a very literal way. Footprints would be suspect. Returning to the garage, she retrieved a plastic carrier bag from the Scalextrix box. Then she walked backward across the yard, smudging her footprints as she went.

Amy watched her.

Inside the house, there were footsteps on the staircase, going down to the floor below. For goodness sake, Nesta, get a move on!

She had to unbolt the yard door, which she and Amy had decided was a minor problem. A little less satisfactory was the mark the door made on the snow as she opened it. Still, that could not be helped. Nesta carried the plastic bag away with her, to be disposed of later. Opening the Browns' wheelie bin was out of the question: that would have disturbed the coating of snow on top of it.

Amy ran to her bedroom door and called down to her mother, "Mum, is that you?"

"And who else would it be?" said her mother, looking up the well of the staircase.

"I don't know," said Amy. "I've had a terrible dream. Someone had broken in and you were fighting them off with Jack's cricket bat, and Dad was lying unconscious 'cos they'd hit him first."

"Come down and have a cup of tea," said her mother, turning toward the kitchen. "I am just going to make one."

"Make sure the front door's shut first," said Amy desperately. "It seemed so real."

Mrs. Brown shrugged, turned to the front door, and gave it a push.

"Satisfied?" she said.

"Maybe it was the cat making a noise," said Amy. "Maybe he's got shut in the cupboard under the stairs."

"Amy Brown!" said her mother in exasperation. "What's got into you? You would think you were three instead of thirteen. Stop being so stupid."

No help for it now. Mum was opening the kitchen door with the ratchet key. Amy was glad that her parents were security conscious. She just wished she had thought of hiding that key! She could have gone down and helped to look for it!

The kitchen door creaked relentlessly open on its unoiled hinges. In seconds the kitchen blind would be raised. . . .

And just in time, only just in time, Nesta closed the yard door behind her.

Amy ran down the stairs and was soon standing behind her mother. She looked out anxiously into the yard and was relieved to see it empty. It was hardly morning, but the snow enhanced the early light.

"Been snowing," said her mother. "I thought it might. It was surely cold enough last night."

She leant forward, looked out the window, and saw the arc of disturbed snow.

"Looks as if we've had someone snooping around," she said irritably. "That back door should have been bolted. I don't know how many times I have to tell you all! No wonder you have nightmares."

"It was probably a tramp," said Amy helpfully. "But he can't have come right in. There are no footprints. He must just have opened the door, looked in, and shut it again."

The lane was deserted. Nesta hurried along it to the main street, which was also quiet at that time on Saturday morning. There wasn't a bus in sight. There wasn't even anyone standing at the bus stop. Nesta made up her mind to walk to the station instead of waiting, though it was quite a long walk. But the train was not due to leave till ten o'clock. She would have plenty of time.

Just before nine o'clock she was passing a television store that had a set switched on in the window. She glanced toward the flickering movement and gasped as she saw her own picture on the local news. She couldn't hear what was being said, but she could guess. Her feelings were in turmoil. *I'll have to keep my head down. I don't want to be taken back too soon. . . . They love me enough to look for me so publicly, at risk to themselves and their secret. . . . Perhaps they have decided not to go. . . .*

Then other thoughts came to her as she hastened to the station. *Perhaps everything has fallen apart. . . . They have gone and it is the authorities that somehow are looking for me, and for them.*

The thought was an abyss that she could not bear to look down into. She felt light-headed and unsteady. It took all her courage to continue to put one foot before the other. She looked down at her feet and thought, quite literally, *One step at a time. That is all I can manage.*

In the station she bought a local morning paper and saw her photograph, all grainy, in the bottom corner of the front page with a short, almost unnoticeable paragraph beneath it:

> **Nesta Gwynn, age twelve, height 5′2″, slim build, light brown hair, gray-blue eyes, has been missing since Wednesday of this week. She is understood to have left home after a disagreement with her parents. They are anxious that she should get in touch, and they assure her that the problem can be sorted out.**

It helped dispel the worst of her doubts, but it was too vague a promise to give her complete reassurance. The only safe proceeding was to stay away until the deadline was past. Besides, whatever happened, she still wanted to meet those people who had known Thomas Derwent. She was determined to extend her knowledge of Ormingat beyond the tight little triangle of herself and her parents.

CHAPTER 27

# Searching for Nesta

Alison half-expected the police to be constantly in touch, even if no news was forthcoming. Yet Friday night passed without any contact.

"I think I'll ring them," she kept saying to Matthew.

"No point," he said. "If they had any news, we would be the first to be told. Things take time."

On Saturday morning, when they looked out to see that it had been snowing overnight, Alison was more distraught than ever. She rang the police station and asked to speak to Sergeant Miller, the officer who had called the day before. He was not on duty. Another voice told her that everything that could be done was being done, and, yes, of course they were taking it seriously. A second voice confirmed that a withdrawal had been made from Nesta's bank account on Wednesday afternoon.

"So you see," said Matthew, "they are doing things, probably more than we know about."

The police really had been busy on the Gwynns' behalf. Quite apart from the visit to the bank, they had also contacted Mrs. Powell and persuaded her to drive down to the school early on Saturday morning to find the address of Nesta's best friend.

"We do appreciate this," said Sergeant Miller. "There is every chance that this friend of hers will be able to give us information. To be honest, I don't think there's any real worry here: the kid'll be hiding out somewhere, making sure she gets her own way."

"What puzzles me," said Mrs. Powell, "is that this is the first I've heard of their going back to Boston. It can't be imminent."

"Kid must have thought it was," said the sergeant, "but you know what they're like at that age. They overreact."

"Amy," called her mother after the policeman on the threshold explained the reason for his visit, "do you know anything about Nesta?"

Amy came along the hall with a feeling of relief that

endowed total innocence. It was nearly noon. Whilst her mother was shopping, with Gerry in tow, Amy had rapidly disposed of the rubbish and returned Grandpa's greatcoat to the wardrobe in the spare room. She had even put Nesta's school clothes in the weekend bag she kept on the floor of her bedroom cupboard. That was a lucky last-minute decision!

She looked suitably puzzled.

"Nesta," she said. "What about Nesta?"

Sergeant Miller looked down at the stocky child, who appeared much younger than he had expected.

"Your friend's gone missing. Her mum and dad are worried about her. Have you any idea where she might be, pet?"

Amy looked at her mother, and then at the policeman.

"I saw her at school on Wednesday," she said, trying her best to avoid the direct lie. "I did think she wasn't feeling well."

"She didn't say she might not be going home?"

"No," said Amy ("might" didn't come into it!). "She just went for her bus the way she always does."

Amy's face reddened, but at the same time her eyes filled with very convincing tears. Her mother put one arm round her shoulders. Nobody said "Was that the last time you saw her?" So there was no need to lie after all.

"I'm sorry we can't help you, Officer," said Mrs.

Brown. "I just hope you find her soon. You will let us know, I hope. Amy and Nesta are very friendly at school. They don't see much of each other out of school, of course; the Gwynns live a fair way from here."

"Would you mind if we have a quick look round the back of the house?" said Sergeant Miller. "We reckon she must have found somewhere to hide out. And it's routine to look at all possibilities, however unlikely, but I reckon you'll know that already."

Mrs. Brown opened the door wider to admit the sergeant and his constable.

"You can look, of course," she said, "but you've heard what Amy said. I doubt if Nesta could sneak in anywhere without her knowing. I am not even sure if she knows where we live."

The two policemen went through to the backyard. They inspected the garage, where a surly-looking young man was busy cleaning his motorbike.

"My son, Jack," said Mrs. Brown, who followed them. "He's home for the weekend."

Jack shrugged his shoulders and went on with what he was doing. That was the cool thing to do. Jack was cool. He had already seen Amy pottering about and had totally ignored her, as she knew he would.

The policemen found no sign of Nesta at all, not in the yard, nor the garage, not even in the karaoke box, which they turned upside down. Amy stood in the kitchen doorway watching, and beneath her look of misery she found it very hard to hide a certain smugness. It was, after all, quite an achievement to have hidden her friend undetected for so long. The misery was genuine too, however, for now she was no longer Nesta's protector. She might have helped her friend into danger. That was an awesome responsibility.

Just after the policemen left, Mrs. Brown remembered the arc of disturbed snow, the evidence of a night intruder.

"I wish I had told them about that tramp," she said. "They should keep a lookout for people like that. I'll have to mention it to the neighborhood watch. Mr. Huddy should be told."

To connect the intruder with the runaway schoolgirl never occurred to her. Amy breathed easy, but her conscience was beginning to supply her imagination with all manner of horrific scenarios. Sunday could not come too soon!

# CHAPTER 28

# Traveling North

Nesta looked up at the station indicator board, saw what platform the train for Casselton would leave from, and made her way across the footbridge to where it was already waiting. She found her seat, a table seat in the corner of the carriage. Then she sat down and looked at the newspaper, carefully folding it so that the front page would not be visible.

Just before the train was about to leave, a plump, elderly lady with a large holdall took the seat opposite. Nesta kept her head down and pulled her hood over her brow. The woman put the holdall on the empty seat next to her and took out her knitting and a pattern for a man's sweater.

"As good a way as any of passing the time," she said, holding up the needles and smiling across at Nesta, who looked up cautiously, saw no real cause for alarm, and gave her fellow traveler a polite little smile. Then she found the crossword in the newspaper, took out her pen, and began to work on the clues.

The ticket collector came past and very quickly checked their tickets, not looking at anything but the pieces of paper thrust at him. *If the police are searching for me,* thought Nesta, *they aren't searching very hard.* When her hood fell back onto her shoulders, she did not bother to pull it back into place.

The train soon left York and its environs behind and was traveling through countryside. Nesta lost heart with the crossword. She looked out of the window at the bleak winter landscape. The day was turning a wishy-washy blue. Suddenly Nesta had tears running down her cheeks and her heart was saying, *I want my mom.*

"Homesick already?" said the old woman, looking at her over her knitting. "Those are homesick tears if ever I saw them. Want to talk?"

Nesta blushed and thought hard what to say. The truth was impossible. So it was necessary to think of a plausible lie.

"I'm going north to see my father," she said. "My parents are divorced. It's his turn to have me this weekend."

"Divorce is a terrible business," said the woman ponderously. "It hurts everyone involved. But you'll find in life that it is not always possible to avoid being hurt. People are always being faced with choices. The only thing to do, I think, is to bear the hurt and hope for better things. Your dad will be pleased to see you. After all, you aren't divorced from either of your parents."

"No," said Nesta, but she found herself thinking, *Ah, but I am. I am divorced from both of them, and they are still married to each other.*

She took out her handkerchief and wiped her eyes.

"That's better," said the woman. "Here, this might help."

From the holdall she drew out a packet of crisps and a small bottle of orange juice. She pushed them across the table to Nesta.

"I always come well prepared. You can't depend on the trolley service these days."

"But you'll want them for yourself," said Nesta.

The woman smiled a nice, jolly smile.

"I've got plenty more if I do," she said, "but I am getting off at Darlington anyway. Not much further."

Nesta sat back and ate the crisps, then drank the orange juice. When they reached Darlington, the woman got up from her seat, then bent over and gave Nesta a quick hug.

"Life's never as bad as it seems, love," she said. She left the carriage, struggling with the bulky holdall. Nesta thought, with adolescent cynicism, *Little do you know, old woman, sometimes it's worse!*

After Darlington Nesta had the table to herself. She rested her head on her arms and dozed. She was hardly aware when the train stopped at signals that had jammed, causing a delay of forty-five minutes. The train had been slow to leave York, slow on its journey north, and this further delay meant that it would not arrive at its destination till half-past one. Some passengers grumbled. Nesta just slept.

*The next stop is Casselton Central Station. This train terminates there. Will passengers please make sure to take all of their luggage with them?*

*We shall be arriving at Casselton Central in five minutes. Passengers are reminded to check their luggage. . . .*

*Thank you for traveling with Great North Eastern Railway.*

Nesta woke with a yawn as the train drew into the station. She looked with surprise at her watch. It was much later than she had expected. There were things she wanted to do in daylight. She left the train quickly and went straight to the station bookstall, where she bought a street map of Casselton. The first thing to do was to find Hedley Crescent.

Before leaving the station, she checked on the times of trains running west to Belthorp and found, to her relief, that most of the Carlisle trains stopped there. At this rate she would be traveling at dusk, but that could not be helped. She would take no risks. She did not intend to go down any back alleys.

# CHAPTER 29

# Suspicious Circumstances

On Saturday afternoon the police received a visit in person from the resident of number 10 Linden Drive. Her high heels clicked on the tiled floor as she came to the desk. The duty officer looked up to see a smartly dressed elderly woman smiling down at him.

"I would like to see whoever is in charge of searching for Nesta Gwynn," she said very precisely. "That's the girl who has gone missing from Linden Drive."

The duty officer nodded.

"Yes, of course," he said. "If you have any information, we would be very pleased to know about it."

He pressed the phone on his desk. A voice answered immediately.

"There's a lady here would like to speak to you about Nesta Gwynn."

The duty sergeant pressed another button on the desk and said, "Just go through that door there, madam. Sergeant Miller will see you."

"Do sit down, Mrs. . . . ?"

"Mrs. Jolly," said the lady as she sat down quite elegantly on the chair in front of the sergeant's desk. "I live next door to the Gwynns. I would have come earlier, but I feel a little foolish about this. It is probably something or nothing. And I do feel treacherous coming here. The Gwynns are such a nice couple. But things do happen, even with nice couples. I mean, they do, don't they?"

"Yes," said the sergeant slowly, "I suppose they do."

Mrs. Jolly seemed to him to be fluttery and unreliable, and he hadn't the faintest idea what she was talking about.

"Just take your time," he said, "and tell me what it is that is worrying you. Have you seen Nesta today, or yesterday maybe?"

"No, no," said Mrs. Jolly. "I haven't seen her all this week. But that's not unusual. I don't often see her. It's just that when I saw on the local news that she was missing, I was niggled by something odd I saw from my bedroom window on Thursday. It baffled me at the time. Now it seems to me that it might even be somehow sinister. I hope you'll tell me I'm stupid. I honestly don't mind being stupid."

"You might be mistaken," said the sergeant, "but there is no way I would say you were stupid. Tell me what you saw and perhaps we can consider it together. Two heads, they say, are better than one."

"Well," said Mrs. Jolly, leaning forward and feeling much more relaxed now that the introduction was over. "I was just closing my bedroom curtains. I always close them before I put the light on, an old habit. My late husband used to insist upon curtains being closed before the lights were switched on. It used to annoy me, but I got so used to it that now I just do it automatically, even though Edward died five years ago. You know how it is—"

Sergeant Miller took the chance to interrupt her.

"So what did you see when you looked out of your window?"

"Them—Mr. and Mrs. Gwynn, out in the back garden, near the pond with that great ugly frog on top of it. They were fiddling around somehow. I couldn't see properly, of course, because our fence is quite high, and then there are the trees at the end of their garden. They are quite old trees, you know, older than any of the houses. I just have one. They have three of them. And we aren't allowed to cut them down: they're protected."

Sergeant Miller plunged in again when she stopped for breath.

"So the Gwynns were out in the garden in the dark engaged in some activity near the old trees?"

"Or the pond," said Mrs. Jolly firmly. "They're always having trouble with that pond. Just last week they had to drain it. But if it weren't there, we might have water coming into our place—I still say our place, even though there's just me now. And the two cats. My son lives in Scotland and, I've got to say it, I hardly ever see him."

"So the Gwynns were down by the pond doing something. Can you be more specific? Did they have spades or anything? Were they carrying any sort of bundle?"

"Not that I could see," said Mrs. Jolly. "Nothing like that. I am not suggesting they were burying a body! Heaven forbid! They seemed to be leaning over and talking. Couldn't hear what they were saying, of course, not through the double-glazing, and you wouldn't want windows open at this time of year, now would you? To be honest with you—and I know this'll sound daft—I thought they were having some weird sort of prayer meeting! Especially when they lit the blue taper and it flared up."

"A blue taper flared up?" said the sergeant. "How do you mean?"

"Just what I say," said Mrs. Jolly. "I mean, I couldn't make anything out properly, but that's what it looked like to me. Then they practically ran into the house, and that was the end of it."

"You saw no more?" said the sergeant.

"I closed the curtains," said Mrs. Jolly primly. "I don't spend my time spying on my neighbors!"

And that, thought Sergeant Miller after Mrs. Jolly left, amounts to what I would call suspicious circumstances.

# CHAPTER 30

# Nesta in Casselton

The map was quite clear; what is more, it even gave bus routes. Nesta found the right bus stop and watched out of the window for Portland Drive, the stop nearest Hedley Crescent. It was only when she got off the bus that she realized that finding James Martin was not going to be absolutely simple. She did not know the house number.

Hedley Crescent was a curved street of terrace houses, each with its own long front garden. Nesta walked the length of it, wondering which one was the Martin house. It was not snowing in Casselton, but it was a very cold afternoon, and so cloudy that it would soon be dusk.

A boy of seven or eight passed her on a scooter. She thought about stopping him but he just whizzed past, almost sending her off-balance. A man was unloading shopping from his car outside number 12. Nesta wanted to ask him if he knew the Martins, but she didn't know what to say. As she passed the gate of number 22, she noticed that the front door was open. She heard a woman calling out, "Jamie, can you not take this dog for a walk? She's standing here with her legs crossed."

The dog was in fact standing on the doorstep, straining at the lead the woman was holding on to.

A boy of ten or eleven came stomping down the stairs inside the house, shouting irritably, "Dad should take her. She's Dad's dog."

Woman, boy, and dog were all on the threshold now.

"Your dad won't be in for another hour. And Calypso is supposed to be your dog anyway."

Jamie took the dog's lead with a "Humph" and started out down the path.

"C'mon, Calypso, we know whose dog you are. But there's no use arguing."

Nesta waited till the boy had gone a few yards down the street before she caught up with him.

"Do you know James Martin?" she said as she drew alongside.

"Who wants to know?" said Jamie, eyeing her suspiciously.

"I do," said Nesta in the same challenging voice.

Jamie looked up at her, a slim stranger in a red hooded coat, taller and older than himself.

"I don't know you," he said doggedly.

"I never said you did," said Nesta. "But do you know James Martin? He'll be about your age and he lives in this street."

"That all you know about him?" said Jamie. The dog began to sniff at Nesta's coat.

"Jamie is short for James, isn't it?" said Nesta, suddenly guessing that the boy was in fact James Martin his very self.

Jamie pulled on Calpyso's lead so that she came closer to him.

"Mind the dog," said Jamie. "She's trained to look after me. She doesn't bark much, but she has a strong pair of jaws when it comes to biting."

"I'm not going to beat you up and take all your money," said Nesta with a grin. "I just want to ask you about your letter in *The Courier*."

Jamie relaxed. After all, he might have to get used to being famous.

"If you want my autograph, I hope you've brought your own pen. I haven't got one with me."

"No, silly," said Nesta. "I am not an autograph hunter. I am a distant relative of your friend Thomas Derwent. I know you only knew him for a short time, but you were quite friendly, weren't you?"

"Kindred spirits," said Jamie, proudly showing off a phrase he'd just learnt. "But you can't be any sort of relative of his. He is special. I know he is. He comes from outer space. You must have heard the stories about him. *You* don't come from outer space. I know you're not from round here, but you are definitely not an alien."

They had come to the end of the crescent. Calypso did her business on the grass verge, and James got out a little old seaside spade and scooped the dirt up into the plastic carrier bag he carried for the purpose. Nesta did not answer him till that performance was over.

"I like dogs," she said. "We only have a cat. Her name is Charlie—short for Charlotte. My dad thinks dogs are too much bother."

"They are," said Jamie ruefully. "You're always having to take them for walks and scoop up after them. But Calypso's not bad really. She sometimes helps me with my homework."

Nesta looked surprised and Jamie laughed.

"It's like this, you see. If I don't get my homework done before Dad comes home, I say I couldn't do it because I had to take Calypso for a walk. Then Dad says, 'Let's have a look at it.' And if it's sums, and it usually is, he can't help doing them, just to show how clever he is."

Nesta laughed and said, "My dad's the same—except I don't even need an excuse. He likes the English questions—that's because he works in a bank and spends all his day working with numbers. English makes a change for him, he says."

Now that they were more friendly, Jamie said, "Well, how come you think you might be related to Thomas Derwent?"

"Distantly related," said Nesta, wondering how much to tell the boy. "He and I might be from the same place originally. What did he tell you?"

"No more than I said in the letter to the paper," said Jamie. "He was fun and we had a laugh, but he didn't talk English. He talked sort of special, in a way of his own. But if you're related to him, you should be able to do it too. Tell me your name."

Nesta realized at once that she could not tell this boy her real name. It might have been on the news even this far north.

"I'm called Amy," she said.

"But what is your proper name?" said Jamie. "Your Ormingat name?"

This time he used the newspaper version of Ormingat, but without any attempt to reproduce the voice that Thomas had used.

"Neshayla," said Nesta in her normal voice, for she had no other! To tell the secret name that her mother had given her seemed harmless here.

"Yah!" said Jamie in disgust. "And my name's Collywolly."

Nesta did not know what to think.

"But my name really is Neshayla. I have been told that. It was entwined with me. *Entwined*—that's what they called it."

Calypso was sitting on the pavement by Jamie's right foot. She stood up and gave herself a brief shake, then pulled at the lead.

"You're right, Calypso," said Jamie. "Better company at home."

"I really, really am Neshayla," said Nesta.

"You haven't a clue, have you?" said Jamie over his shoulder as he walked away. "If you were Thomas Derwent's cousin or whatever, you'd know how to speak in the voice. You've read the papers and you're just plain nosy."

Nesta then remembered the voice her mother had used, a voice she could not hope to imitate. So it was true: Thomas Derwent really did come from Ormingat. And the voice her mother had used was the voice of that distant world. There was no more to be found out here. That was obvious. The boy was heading toward his own house.

"See you sometime," called Nesta as she walked off in the opposite direction.

"Not if I see you first," said Jamie, kicking a stray piece of gravel into the roadway as he walked away. The dog said nothing, but tugged harder on the lead and began to sniff at the ground.

Nesta was alarmed to notice that, although it was still not three o'clock, it was already getting dark. She hurried back to the bus stop and had ten minutes to wait for the bus to Casselton Central Station. It was shivery cold.

In the station she was dismayed to find that the next train was not until half-past four. That would mean arriving in Belthorp well after dark.

At four o'clock, as she went to the platform for the Belthorp train, she bucked herself up with the thought that in ten hours' time she would be able to phone home and give herself up. *Because Mom and Dad will be there, of course.* There was no way they would leave without her. That was a belief she must cling to. If she could persevere in that a little bit longer, a few more hours, they could all live happily ever after.

*I am doing what is best for them. I am doing what is best for all of us.*

In the meantime, she was determined to see Belthorp and somehow to meet Mrs. Dalrymple, who had known Thomas for five years. What was this "starlight" she had spoken about? Did it come from Ormingat? Was it something Thomas had left behind?

CHAPTER 31

# Further Inquiries

From the front window of the house in Linden Drive, Alison looked out into near darkness. Smears of snow lingered in corners of the garden from last night's fall. Orange streetlamps made the empty road look bleak and lonely.

*Where are you now, Nesta? What are you doing this dreary afternoon?*

Alison was just about to close the curtains and shut out the cheerless scene when, suddenly, a police car came round the corner into their street. She watched it draw up outside the front gate, and then hurried to the door.

"What is it?" she said anxiously as Sergeant Miller stood before her. "Have you heard anything?"

"Not really, Mrs. Gwynn. But we need to talk to you," said the policeman. "Can we come in?"

"Certainly," said Alison.

Matthew was hurrying down the stairs, momentarily hopeful. But it was clear from everyone's expression that nothing good had happened.

"What we need to know," said Sergeant Miller as they sat down in the front room, "is why you were busy in the garden quite late on Thursday afternoon. I mean, it is an odd time of year and time of day to be out doing the garden. I am sure you have an explanation."

Matthew looked puzzled.

"I don't know what you mean," he said. "Of course we weren't out doing the garden on Thursday afternoon, or anytime at all on Thursday."

"I thought as much," said the policeman. "But you were doing something out there and, to be honest with you, I'd be easier in my mind if I knew what it was."

"We really don't understand you, Sergeant Miller," said Alison. "What would we be doing that could be of any interest to you? You are searching for our daughter. We checked the garden thoroughly on Wednesday night and again on Thursday morning. We thought she might have made herself a hiding place behind the trees, though it didn't seem very likely."

"Yes," said the sergeant, "that's what I mean. Like you, we have to explore every possible avenue, however unlikely it might appear to be. Think back now—were you in the garden at all on Thursday evening? Your neighbor thought she saw you out there. I don't think she was being malicious or anything. She's just an elderly woman living alone and I suppose she gets nervous."

Then Alison realized what he was talking about and what Mrs. Jolly had seen them doing: consulting the communicator by lifting the frog and calling down to the ship! Oh dear, explaining that would surely be impossible. She was struck dumb. There just wasn't an explanation that would divert attention from the one area that needed protection. She tried hard to summon up the power that had helped her deal with Amanda's bullying and Nesta's shock; but the power was weakened, almost gone. As the sergeant looked into her eyes, he saw nothing there but fear and misery. The only spell was silence, and it was Matthew who broke it.

"*I* remember," he said, giving Alison a rueful glance. "I remember now. We were quarreling about whether or not to call you in to look for Nesta. I thought it was too soon. My wife was all for calling you there and then. She began to cry and ran out into the back garden. I followed her and talked her into being calm and coming back into the house."

"What about the blue light?" said the sergeant. That was a startling question.

"A tad scary," said Matthew, taking a deep breath. "I suppose it would frighten Mrs. Jolly too. There was a single flash of lightning, and then the heavens opened and it began to pour."

"So you ran back into the house?"

"Yes, we did. And even so, we both got drenched."

It was an explanation. Sergeant Miller was not sure that he was entirely satisfied with it. Why were they not more annoyed with their neighbor for talking about them? Indignation would have been natural.

"We're used to Mrs. Jolly, you know," said Matthew, as if reading the sergeant's mind. "She tends to imagine things. She's quite harmless."

Alison offered the sergeant and his constable a cup of tea, which they accepted and sat comfortably drinking as they talked about the neighborhood, the weather, and the hope that Nesta would soon be safe.

"No news is good news, after all," said the sergeant, and for once he really meant it. For reasons he could not pinpoint, it suddenly seemed to him that there would be no dead body at the end of this case. For reasons she could easily pinpoint, Alison shared his optimism. Some relic of the power of Ormingat was stirring in her and secretly informing her that all was not lost.

"She'll be home tomorrow," she said with confidence. "I feel sure she will."

"I hope you're right, Mrs. Gwynn," said the sergeant as he put his cup and saucer back on the tray and got up to leave. "We'll be off now. As soon as anything happens we'll be in touch."

As they were getting into the car, Mrs. Jolly came furtively along the road, approaching the vehicle from the offside, furthest away from the Gwynns' gate.

"What is it, Mrs. Jolly?" said the constable as he wound down the window.

"They move that frog, you know," she said. "It takes the two of them to do it, but I have seen them do it before. They shift it right out onto the lawn. Not on Thursday, mind you, but it was quite dark then and not easy to see. That was something I forgot to tell you."

"Thank you, Mrs. Jolly," said Sergeant Miller. "You've been very helpful."

They drove off, leaving their informant to scuttle back to her own drive.

 When they got to the main road, Sergeant Miller was troubled with second thoughts.

"Maybe we should have checked the frog," he said.

"I was wondering about that," said the constable.

"And the passports," mused the sergeant.

"They could do a runner overnight," said the constable. "Maybe that's why they seemed less worried."

203

"I'll ask for a watch on the house tonight, I think," said the sergeant. "I don't want to go back there now. If the girl doesn't turn up tomorrow, we'll have to take it further. If it really is serious, it won't be our job then."

# CHAPTER 32

# Belthorp

The station at Belthorp was hardly a station at all: no W. H. Smith, no Burger King, nothing but railway lines between two platforms and a footbridge over them. It was more of a halt really.

For the past half hour, Nesta had been able to see nothing from the window but her own reflection. The carriage was brightly lit and about half full of passengers. She had a terrible feeling that everything was becoming much harder than she had ever imagined. She had thought to arrive at Belthorp in daylight, with plenty of time to find Mrs. Dalrymple, and even to return to Casselton, if necessary, and board a late train going south. She had not bargained for slow trains and long delays.

At Belthorp only half a dozen alighted. Nesta

followed them over the footbridge. Those in a hurry were soon out of sight; a mother and her little boy went more slowly, as did a strange-looking man in a long dark overcoat. Nesta made up her mind to stay as close as possible to the woman and child. The man in the dark overcoat was tall but hunched in a furtive way. Round his neck, with one long end dangling down his back, was a white scarf ending in silky tassels. It was the scarf that was most off-putting. It looked so out of place and eccentric.

All four passengers emerged from the station to-gether. Nesta's heart sank when the woman and child got straight into a waiting car. The man walked quite slowly to a spot further down the road, then stopped. Out in the darkness of a damp, foggy evening, Nesta stood still and did not know which way to go. The road to her left, where the man was standing, sloped gently downward, as if toward a valley. To her right the same road went more steeply uphill.

As Nesta looked up the hill, a single-decker country bus trundled into sight. The destination panel said BELTHORP. The bus drew into the bus stop where the man was standing. So that was what he was standing for! Nesta hurried toward the bus, reaching it just af-ter two passengers had alighted.

"After you, my dear," said the man in the overcoat, standing back to let her pass. He smiled with a smile that showed too many very even teeth. His face was dark and foreign looking. Nesta mumbled thanks and jumped on the bus. The man followed.

Nesta took coppers from her pocket and said, "The center of Belthorp, please."

It didn't sound quite right but she knew no other way to phrase it.

The driver gave her a curious look, then said, "That'll be the Green, pet. You'll not be wanting to go to the terminus."

He charged her a half-fare without query. The man behind her bought a ticket to the Green. Nesta was pleased to see that there were other passengers on the bus. She hoped that some of them would get off at the Green.

The first stop was at the end of a row of cottages. This was Merrivale, where Mrs. Dalrymple lived, but Nesta did not know that. Several people descended there, leaving the bus nearly empty.

"The Green," said the driver loudly as he drew into the next stop. He looked back to make sure that his young passenger had heard.

Nesta got up and left the bus. The man followed.

In the darkness, made worse by the fog, Nesta made out a wide expanse of grass with houses beyond some trees at the far side. Behind her was a row of stone buildings with steps up to their doors. The nearest one had a black horse on a sign over the doorway. The bank.

Further away, in the direction where the bus had gone, was the steeple of a church, signs of a church-yard, and a dark alleyway leading off just before it.

"Are you lost, love?" said the man, coming up behind her and looking over her shoulder.

Nesta jumped. Way down the road was the block of shops the bus had passed. One of them still seemed to be open, with lights struggling through the fog. But it was too far away to offer any protection. No one was anywhere near.

Nesta turned to face the stranger.

"No, I am not lost. I am meeting a friend here. I'll just have to wait."

"There's a bench over there," said the man. "As cheap to sit as to stand."

For a moment, Nesta had the terrible thought that the man was going to offer to keep her company. She gave him a look of extreme terror.

The man looked back at her and laughed.

"I don't eat little girls, you know," he said. "I am an extremely well-fed monster."

He turned away and walked on into the back alley, where, though Nesta did not know it, his wife and children were eagerly awaiting his return home.

Nesta watched him go, and then was glad to take his advice. She sat on the bench to think. But what thoughts, what dreadful thoughts on a cold, dark night!

What on earth was she doing there, searching for a woman she had never met, hoping for solutions to an insoluble problem? Sadness took over and her mind became a maze of muddled thoughts.

*I have a broken heart.*

It seemed to her that her heart had turned brittle and shattered into sharp pieces, crunching into themselves like glass, inflicting terrible pain on her rib cage. And it was true. Where her heart should have been there was the deepest hurt.

Her head, of its own accord, bent forward onto her hands and she sobbed.

"Mom, oh, Mom, why have I come to this?"

She tried to stop crying, but the tears of days had burst out and would not be dammed.

"Please, God, help me," she cried. "Somebody help me."

At that moment Nesta heard footsteps approaching. She drew herself back and rubbed her eyes with her sleeves. She looked furtively toward the path to see who was coming and sighed with relief when she saw it was just a boy of her own age, possibly younger. He was hurrying along with a plastic carrier bag in his hand.

As he came to the bench, he gave Nesta what seemed to be no more than a glance as he passed, but it was a perceptive glance. Mickey Trent, though only eleven, was born to care about people. He cared most about his mother, but that did not exclude anyone else who might seem in need of help. Mickey walked just a few yards before turning back.

"Are you all right?" he said, looking down at Nesta.

"Yes," said Nesta tersely. Then she looked up at Mickey and crumbled.

"No," she said, "I'm not all right. I am in dreadful trouble and I don't know what to do."

Mickey came and sat on the bench beside her, quite deferentially, and not too close. The plastic carrier bag was on the seat between them. It was full of books.

"Can I get help for you? Is there anybody here you know?"

With one hand he indicated the peripheries of the village.

"I'm trying to find Mrs. Dalrymple," said the girl more hopefully.

"That's easy," said Mickey. "She just lives over there."

He pointed diagonally at the row of cottages way over the west of the Green.

"That's Merrivale," he said. "She lives at number twelve. My best friend used to live at number thirteen."

Nesta looked at him curiously.

"Do you know Thomas Derwent?" she said.

"That's him," said Mickey. "He's the one used to live at number thirteen, before he went."

"Where did he go?" said Nesta.

"Away," said Mickey, "right away from here."

"He's the boy who disappeared, isn't he?"

"Yes," said Mickey, sealing his lips on the word.

"I think I might be distantly related to him," said Nesta.

"You couldn't be," said Mickey spontaneously.

Nesta might have given a longer argument in return, full of invented circumstantial evidence, but she didn't. She just looked directly at Mickey and held his gaze.

"I could," she said firmly, "and I think I am."

Mickey gasped as he understood what she was saying. Then he sneezed hard, further proof, if needed, that the girl was somehow part of the mystery that he and Mrs. Dalrymple had silently shared these past weeks.

"I think you should go to Mrs. Dalrymple's now," said Mickey. "She knows more than I do. And my mam'll be getting worried. I've just been to Auntie Fay's for her library books. I'll have to be getting home. I'll walk with you to Mrs. Dalrymple's door, if you come now. It's on my way."

Nesta rubbed her eyes again, got up from the seat, slung her bag on her shoulder, and felt the beginnings of optimism. The worst was surely over.

They went through the white gate into the little garden. Mickey rang the doorbell. A light went on inside, and then the door opened.

"What is it, Mickey?" said Mrs. Dalrymple, looking down at the boy and glancing at the girl standing there beside him.

"This is a friend of Thomas's," he said. "She came here to see you, but she didn't know where you lived. She says she's related to Thomas. She wants to talk to you. I don't think she's from the papers or anything."

And, true enough, the girl did not have the appearance of a reporter or a snoopy investigator!

"Come in, the two of you," said Mrs. Dalrymple, holding the door wide. "We can talk about it over a cup of tea."

"I can't," said Mickey. "I'll have to get home. My mam'll just start worrying if I don't."

Stella Dalrymple smiled. Mickey's mam was a famous worrier!

Mickey gave her a wave as he hurried off home.

"Well, come in . . . ?" she said to Nesta, the raised voice clearly asking for a name.

"I'm Nesta," said the girl.

"And I'm Stella," said Mrs. Dalrymple. "Come on in and tell me all about it."

# CHAPTER 33

# A Strange Farewell

The policemen had gone.

Alison and Matthew were left alone in a house that somehow vibrated with all the trouble that swirled about it. In the back garden, beneath the frog, the spaceship's communicator was working furiously, sending out signals to the house. Ormingat does not readily give up on its people.

There was even an Ormingat search going on for Nesta, but the girl was impossible to find. There was nothing there to hold on to, no way of reaching out and talking to her. Matthew and Alison knew that only too well. Nesta was truly a child of the Earth, unschooled in any lore of Ormingat.

Upstairs in the Gwynn house, the clock radio grated out the words, "Come-to-the-source. Take-heed-of-time.

Beware-of-ending." This went on for the best part of an hour, until the equipment paused for breath. It was a makeshift line of communication, not designed for such a use.

Downstairs, the Gwynns never heard it. But they felt a pull toward the rear of the house that they resisted with all their might. They intended to remain on Earth for the sake of their daughter, but they knew that their real place at that moment was in the ship and they were fighting not only against the outside force, but against the feeling inside themselves. *We are of Ormingat and not of Earth. Without the ship, that will be our loss forever.*

The clock on the mantelpiece beat time loudly.

At midnight Matthew said, "Best if we go to bed. I know we won't sleep, but at least it is the natural place to be at this hour. We can lie in the darkness and wait for the time to pass."

"But what will happen when the spaceship leaves? How will it leave? Will it not be seen shooting up into the sky?"

"Too small," said Matthew. "It will travel like a spark out into the darkness, never to be seen again."

One thing they had forgotten was the frog. The bulky stone frog was squatting on top of the spaceship's flight path. It was only when they were lying in bed that Alison thought of the problem.

"What about the frog?" she said. "Even though we

ourselves are not leaving, maybe we should have emptied the pond and moved the frog. It was empty when we first arrived. We had to figure out what to do with the frog that was lying on the lawn. We even had to find the valve to fill the pond."

"Stop worrying, Allie," said Matthew, yawning. "The power of Ormingat is strong enough to pass through anything, even stone. Departure is much simpler than arrival. They are masters of illusion, remember. Their science is way in advance of anything on this Earth. Atoms will split for them, split and rejoin. They know what they are doing."

"You give them too much credit," said Alison bitterly. "They could not find our daughter. *We* don't really know what they can or cannot do."

"Perhaps they didn't want to find her," said Matthew. "It could be that they are somehow inhibited by her wish not to be found."

To that, Alison could find no answer.

At one o'clock in the morning, the radio, which had fallen silent some time before the Gwynns came to their room, suddenly began to buzz again. Matthew started up. Alison grasped his arm. They listened.

"Time-is-gone." The radio's grating sound was huskier, almost as if filled with emotion. "The-door-is-closed. You-are-lost-to-us-for-all-time."

Then came a sound as of muffled weeping.

"Closed-door. Time-gone. You-lost." The radio spoke more tersely, sounding unutterably sad.

The accent had changed, slightly but perceptibly. The machine, which was after all just a machine, was suddenly conveying a deep emotion. It was as if their parents and their grandparents were sending one last message out to them.

Matthew and Alison heard it and were filled with grief and guilt and doubt. *Are we losing too much for a child who might already be lost?* They shared the thought and sighed deeply, still watching the clock radio as its digits ticked off the minutes.

"No-more-can-we-do. We-love-you. We-always-love-you."

Then the voice went dead and the digits on the clock blanked out. Time was passing. To the absolute limit of Ormingat ability, the strange farewell had been said.

"We have lost them . . . or they have lost us," said Matthew. There had been no last-minute reprieve. If, at that moment, the chance had been offered, he might even have returned to Ormingat alone.

Alison sighed, feeling more for him than with him. Yes, undeniably yes, the loss was great, but for her there was an emotion even more important that weakened the impact of the mournful voice. *My child means more than a myriad of ancestors.*

"I need Nesta," she said. "Tomorrow, oh, tomorrow, when she returns to us, we'll learn to cope with our other loss. Nothing matters more to me than the return of our daughter."

Matthew could not speak.

Now that the clock was dead, he needed to look at his watch to see the time. Just as he switched on the bedside lamp and saw that the fatal hour of two was almost there, a gigantic explosion shook the house.

Windows rattled.

Plaster cracked inside the walls.

The sound of a high-pitched whistle invaded their ears.

"What on earth can that be?" cried Alison.

"The ship!" said Matthew, grabbing his dressing gown and dashing to the bedroom door. "The spaceship has had to burst out of its confinement. We should have moved the frog."

But from the back bedroom window, he could see nothing. The garden was in deep darkness. He and Alison ran downstairs and out into the night. They rushed up to the pond. The grass around it was wet. The basin was empty of water, but spattered with bits of masonry, leaves broken off from the lily pad.

The frog was nowhere in sight.

# CHAPTER 34

# Stella and Nesta

"You look perished," said Stella as she took a very grateful and almost tearful Nesta into the sitting room with its crackling fire and cozy armchairs.

"I'll take your coat. Put this rug round you till you warm up," said Stella, "and I'll go and make you a warm drink. Tea? Chocolate?"

Nesta handed over her coat and said, "Tea, please," in a voice that was almost mechanical. The contrast between the cold misery of the bench on the Green and the warmth and comfort of this little house was too great to digest straightaway. Stella guided her to the armchair and draped the tartan travel rug round her shoulders. First things first: Stella did not know who this child might be or why she was there, but she knew at a glance that here were misery and discomfort that needed instant care.

"Would you like some soup? I've only got vegetable and it is tinned, but it would warm you up," called Stella from the other room. "Nice fresh rolls, though—I can pop them in to warm."

She appeared in the doorway and waited for her visitor to give a reply.

"I'd love some," said Nesta, her eyes grayer than ever and brimming with tears again. It wasn't the misery that was making her tearful now, it was the warmth of the room and the sweet relief of having this lovely fairy godmother of a lady suddenly there to look after her.

"That's right," said Stella briskly. "Nothing's broken that can't be mended."

That made her guest feel almost cheerful.

"I'll put the TV on for you if you like. Just the news, but it's company."

"No," said Nesta quickly. "Please no. I'll just sit and watch the fire."

Stella smiled and went back to the kitchen, not suspecting that Nesta had good reasons for not wanting to see the news. There was that image she had seen in the TV shop window: herself onscreen, a missing person. Nesta would have explanations enough to make without the added burden of facing up to whatever was being said about her on the television.

Mickey Trent gasped when he saw Nesta's picture. He and his mother were sitting with supper trays watching *The Northern News*.

"What is it?" said his mother. Jenny Trent had heard the gasp and was instantly worried in case something was wrong.

"Nothing," said Mickey. "Just a hot chip."

*So*, he was thinking, *the girl's parents have reported her disappearance to the police*. What did that mean? Should he tell, should he say he had seen her? It was dilemma time again—Mickey was learning that life is full of difficult decisions.

*Leave it to Mrs. Dalrymple*, said his heart. *Tell no one*.

That was enough: Mickey's heart was always in the right place, a fact his head was quick to recognize.

"There now," said Stella as she brought in the tray, "hot soup, warm rolls, and a nice mug of tea."

She set the tray down on the coffee table and sat down facing Nesta.

"Thank you so much, Stella," said the girl. She took a sip of the tea and felt its warmth inside her. The rug slipped from her shoulders but she did not need it now.

"You'll be wondering . . . ," she began, faltering, as she broke a roll in two and dipped it in the hot soup.

"I am," said Stella with a smile, "but I can wait until you're fed and comfortable. It's impossible to tell a good story on an empty stomach."

Nesta was well satisfied with that. It gave her time to think.

"Well," said Stella after they had sat quietly for some minutes, "perhaps I should start first. My name is Stella Dalrymple, and I have lived here in this village for most of my life. For five years I had these lovely neighbors called Derwent. The father was Patrick. His son was Thomas, who you think might be a relative of yours."

"Not quite a relative exactly," said Nesta uneasily. "It's more complicated than that."

Stella could see that her visitor was struggling to find words. The girl looked so tired it was all Stella could do not to say, "I'll make up the bed in the spare room; we'll talk tomorrow when you've had a good sleep." But she couldn't do that. Here was a girl of twelve or thirteen maybe, brought in from the cold like a poor, sick animal. Her parents, or whoever had charge of her, must surely be frantic. It was only the Thomas connection that stopped Stella lifting the telephone there and then and talking to the police.

"I have to know where you are from," said Stella carefully. "You are a young girl alone in a strange place on a dark evening. I suspect your parents don't know where you are. And if they don't, they will be very worried. Have you run away from home?"

The direct question was accompanied by a very direct look straight into the girl's eyes. And the answer was there: of course she had run away.

"Why?" said Stella. She put her cup down on the coffee table, leant forward earnestly, clasped Nesta's hands in hers, and waited for an answer.

"It's hard to explain," said Nesta. "There are things I can't tell you because I am not supposed to tell. I have been specially told not to tell. In any case, they are things you would never believe. No one would. You would think I was mad, or telling lies."

"Let's start by you telling me as much as you can," said Stella gently.

"If I tell you enough to guess," said Nesta tentatively, "you must never tell anybody else."

"I am not sure that I can promise that," said Stella. "If you have done something illegal or very wrong, I would have to tell. But if it is what I half-think it is, then maybe I have already guessed. And I have already stayed silent. Exchange a secret for a secret?"

Nesta nodded.

"Well, I'll begin. And my secret has to start with a story about a little boy, just six years old, who came into my life with his father and who told me what seemed to be the most outrageous lies."

Nesta looked interested. She knew all about stories that sounded fantastic. She felt she was part of one.

"What did he tell you?" she said.

"It was lovely," said Stella. "He sat where you are sitting now and told me that he was from another planet and had traveled here in a ship the size of a golf ball."

Nesta blushed deeply. That was just too near the truth.

"Only," said Stella, "it wasn't a lie. It was the absolute truth, though it took me five years to find it out. And by then Thomas and his father had set out in their ship for their own planet, leaving traces behind that I alone could interpret. That, I believe, was them saying a loving farewell to me. So, Nesta, a secret for a secret. It is your turn to tell me yours."

# nesta and Stella

Nesta looked searchingly at Stella. How was she to understand her? How was she to be understood? This was a woman older than her mother, yet not really old at all. Her hair was a curious coppery color. Her eyes seemed a shade of amber. Her smile was warm but quiet.

"Before I tell you," said Nesta, "there is one great and important favor I have to ask."

"Yes?" said Stella. She stooped to take a log from the scuttle and put it on the fire. Her manner was unhurried. She would take time to listen.

"Please," said Nesta, "can I stay with you till tomorrow morning, and will you tell no one about me?"

"I don't know whether I can," said Stella. "Someone, somewhere is bound to be looking for you. It seems almost criminal not to let them know that you are safe. Whatever I can do, I will."

"Amy didn't tell," said Nesta. "She's my best friend and she's very hard to convince if she thinks anything is wrong. She told the teachers when I was bullied at school, even though I begged her not to. But she hasn't told my parents where I am now because I managed to make her understand how important it was to keep quiet."

"You told Amy about Ormingat?" said Stella, showing just how much she had already guessed, and worried at how far the secret now had spread. The thought of Rupert Shawcross clumsily checking a new visitation was not a pleasant one.

"No," said Nesta. "I just told her that my parents had decided to go to Boston immediately. The bit she had to accept was that if they did not go this week, they would never go at all. I told her I couldn't explain it but that it was true."

"There was a deadline then for leaving?"

"Yes," said Nesta. "If they do not go at two o'clock tomorrow morning, they will never be able to go at all."

"So," said Stella, "let me understand this. You need to stay away till that hour has passed."

Nesta nodded.

"Then it would surely be possible to ring your parents straight after two o'clock. There will be no need to wait till morning. But that still leaves everyone hours of worrying. I really don't know, Nesta, what I should do. Convince me."

Nesta's expression was one of desperation.

"If you don't help me, I don't know where to turn. I was born in England and I have lived here all my life. There is no way I would risk being taken away to some-place I can't even picture. Did Thomas not feel like that?"

"I don't think so," said Stella. "He loved me and I loved him. For five years I took care of him. But when it came to the point, he could not bear to be parted from his father. And, unlike you, he must have had some knowledge of Ormingat: he would surely have been born there."

"I love my mom and dad," said Nesta, "but not enough to leave the Earth with them. That makes me less loyal than Thomas, doesn't it? But that's not how I feel. I suppose I am depending on them loving me enough not to go without me."

"And if they do?" said Stella. "After all, it will be a hard choice for them."

"If they do, I'll have no one. So I have to be sure, sure, sure that they won't."

Yet there remained a doubt that a hundred *sures* could not dispel.

"If they are not there tomorrow," whispered Nesta guiltily, "you will have to hand me over to the police.

They are looking for me. That is why I did not want you to see the TV tonight."

"That makes it even worse," said Stella. "The police are already very dubious of me. It would be better for all of us if no connection were made. Just sit quiet and let me think."

Stella poured herself a second cup of tea and offered one to Nesta, who refused. In the silence that followed, the clock on the mantelpiece could be heard ticking and the logs in the hearth seemed to crackle more loudly.

"Stay the night," said Stella at length. "At ten past two, I shall phone your parents and tell them you are safe. But the police must be kept out of it, for everybody's sake."

"Oh, thank you!" said Nesta. "Thank you."

Then she added, almost as if to reassure, "If we told them all the truth, you know, they would never believe it. Nobody would. So I don't think it's as important as all that."

"It is," said Stella. "The policemen would not believe any of it, but there are those who would want to check it out. For you to know me, for my name to appear anywhere near yours, is dangerous. There are people on this planet whose job it is to find out all they can about visitors like you."

"I am not a visitor," said Nesta. "I was never a visitor.

Earth is where I was born. I belong here. And here is where I am going to stay."

Her words ended in a yawn. Then her eyes could stay open no longer. She slumped sideways on her chair in a deep sleep, just like a baby.

"Poor child," said Stella. She bent over, lifted Nesta up in her arms, and laid her gently on the sofa. Nesta gave another yawn, tried to wake up, but couldn't. Three nights in the garage and a long day on the road here, followed by this difficult discussion, had simply drained all her strength. Stella tucked the tartan travel rug round her and left her to sleep.

It was after nine o'clock when Nesta stirred again. She looked round in bewilderment and had to try hard to remember where she was. She was alone in the room. Stella was next door washing the dishes.

"Hello," called Nesta in a timid, worried voice.

"I'm here," said Stella, coming straight in at the sound. "Feel better for your sleep?"

"What time is it?" said Nesta, rubbing her eyes.

"Ten past nine," said Stella. "Now, if you can wake up for a little while, there's a comfortable bed upstairs you can sleep in. I've got it all aired and ready."

"You haven't told anybody?" said Nesta.

Stella smiled.

"I couldn't, could I? I'm as deep in the mud as you're in the mire!"

Nesta managed a smile at the strange expression. She had never heard it before, but she could guess what it meant.

"Now then," said Stella. "You do trust me. So as soon as you feel like it, you can go to bed and sleep till morning. I will phone your parents at ten past two—that's just five hours from now—and I will make arrangements to take you home tomorrow. All *you* have to do is catch up on your sleep."

"What if they don't answer?" said Nesta, facing up to a very real worry.

"They will," said Stella.

"But what if they don't?" Nesta persisted. "What if . . . what if they've gone?"

"They won't have," said Stella firmly. "Let's not even think about it. There are some bridges much better left until we come to them."

In the next hour, Nesta drank chocolate and told Stella the whole of her story, not even omitting Grandpa Turpin's greatcoat. Then she went comforted to bed.

No one could offer greater security than Stella Dalrymple. She was not a fairy godmother. But she possessed all the qualities required for the job! At ten past two in the morning, she rang the number Nesta had given her.

There was no answer.

Stella let the phone ring for ten long minutes before replacing the receiver. Then she sat back and wondered what on earth she could do. What a useless instrument a telephone is if there is no one at the other end to answer it!

What was she to tell the girl upstairs, exhausted but sleeping in the hopes of everything being right by morning?

*I do that to people,* thought Stella, impatient with herself. *I convince them that I can put everything right. You'd think I'd know by now that I can't. I was depending on the Gwynns not leaving without their daughter; but I don't know them and I don't know how strong a pull their own planet has on them. . . .*

*If they are gone, I shall have somehow to pick up the pieces. I might not be much good at it, but there isn't anybody else. Tell the police. Arrange for Nesta to stay here with me, at least for a time. And, if necessary, lie through my teeth!*

Her hand went toward the receiver. *The child reported missing from home in York is here in my house. I took her in because she was lost and frightened. I have settled her down for the night. Can we leave her asleep till morning?*

The hand hesitated as Stella mulled over what she would say. Then the thought came that perhaps the parents had not left after all. Perhaps they were even now out looking for Nesta. *One of them should have stayed at home to answer the phone,* she thought crossly. *They'll be running round like headless chickens, getting nowhere.*

*I'll wait awhile,* she thought as the wave of irritation passed. She could understand how those parents were feeling. She just knew what sort of panic they would be in.

*I'll try again later, one more try.*

*And if there is still no reply, what can I do?*

*Cross that bridge when you come to it, Stella Dalrymple!*

# CHAPTER 36

# Where the Frog Went

It was as well the police car was parked at a safe distance on the other side of Linden Drive. It was as well that no late-night reveler was walking home along the pavement outside number 8 on this cold but quiet night.

For suddenly there was an explosion, perhaps it would be better to say a detonation, as if a great cannon had been fired. What followed seemed even more primitive. The startled policemen looked up to see a stone of huge size fall from the sky into the road. Like a missile flung from a medieval trebuchet, the frog had come hurtling high over the roof of the house into the front street. As it hit the ground, it split into three large lumps that became bouncing bombs hammering holes in the roadway. One hit a main and sent a jet of water whizzing up into the air.

After a few seconds that seemed like forever, the constables in the car recovered enough to call for help, lots and lots of help. In a sort of hysteria, they asked for emergency backup, the fire brigade, an ambulance, and anything else that might be on hand. Fortunately, or unfortunately, it was a quiet night in York. There was an eagerness to answer this frantic summons.

"You stay here, Andy," said the constable in the passenger seat, after the call had been made and answered. "I'll go round the back of the house and see what I can see."

Before he was halfway up the Gwynns' front path, bells and horns could be heard as all the might of York's emergency services gathered from different directions to come to the rescue. The constable continued round to the back garden, comforted by the knowledge that he would not be alone for long.

What did he expect to find there? Evidence of an earthquake? Signs that some unsuspected dormant volcano had erupted? No, strangely enough, he had this odd thought that there might be some gigantic catapult set up on the back lawn. He had the makings of a good policeman!

He was really quite disappointed to find Matthew

and Alison Gwynn gazing speechlessly at a hole in the ground, with not a siege engine in sight.

"What happened?" he said.

"We don't know," said Matthew. "We heard this loud bang and came out here to see what it was. But we're none the wiser. Except the frog's gone."

"The frog?"

"There was a huge ornamental frog sitting on the lily pad," said Alison, "a really ugly object, been there since we moved in. Whenever we cleaned the pond it took two of us to move it. Now it isn't here."

"Whew!" said the policeman. "I think I can tell you where it is. Not five minutes ago, a great block of stone flew over your roof, landed in the front street, and broke into pieces."

The fire engine came speeding round the corner of Linden Drive at that moment, followed by two police cars, an ambulance, and a medic on a motorbike. Doors and windows were flung open all over the street. The constable, Matthew, and Alison looked at one another appalled. It seemed to each of them that, mysterious though the blast had been, it was about to receive a disproportionate amount of attention.

"Nobody hurt?" said the constable, knowing what the answer would be.

"Not back here," said Matthew. "What about at the front?"

"Burst water main, but there wasn't anybody round to get hurt," said the constable. Then, remembering that he was supposed to be watching this house and this couple very discreetly, he added, "We just happened to be passing; good job we weren't too close."

Detective Inspector Stirling took charge. Inquiries had now moved on to a much higher and more serious level.

What was needed was done and peace was restored. Then, and only then, the inspector turned his attention to the Gwynns, who by now were standing out in the front street watching the proceedings.

Inside the empty house, the phone rang quite insistently for at least ten minutes, but no one was there to hear it.

"I think we should go indoors, Mrs. Gwynn," said the inspector. He was very soft-spoken but his manner was that of one in authority. He ushered both of the Gwynns toward the house.

"Back way," said Matthew. "That's the way we came, and I haven't brought a front-door key."

In the back garden, two policemen and an officer from the fire service were still busy inspecting the hole where the frog had been.

"Any ideas yet?" asked Inspector Stirling as they passed.

"None at all. We'll have to work on the theory that there has been a buildup of underground gas," said the man from the fire service.

"A natural accident?"

"Not much else it could be, is there?"

Inspector Stirling shook his head.

"I suppose not," he said, "but it seems odd that it should happen to this couple at just this time, when their young daughter has mysteriously disappeared."

"What do you mean?" said the fire officer.

"Well," said the inspector slowly. "I wondered rather whether it might not have been an accident at all. Could it have been in any way deliberate? Could someone somehow have caused it?"

"Practically impossible, I should think," said the fire officer. Then he added, "But, to be honest with you, the natural accident will take a fair amount of explaining too."

Matthew and Alison were already ahead of the inspector going into the house. His conversation with the fire officer was not quite audible to them, but the words *natural accident* registered with Matthew. It would be the most useful and least embarrassing explanation. Any hint that this might be due to extraterrestrial activities would be terrible. *Especially now that we have burnt our boats!*

"That pond has always been a trouble," he said to the inspector as they entered the house. "Just last week

I had to drain it because it had got choked and was overflowing."

They went into the front room and sat down. The inspector did not sit in a comfortable armchair, but instead chose a hard, high-back chair as distant as possible from Mr. and Mrs. Gwynn. His appearance was so nondescript that people found it difficult to remember what he looked like. He had no charm and no desire to please.

"The explosion, or whatever it was, is now the concern of the scientists, those wonderful forensic people who can see a world in a grain of sand," he said in his quiet, slightly sarcastic voice.

Alison shivered at the words. What did he know about grains of sand to speak so glibly? Now that she was committed to humanity, it seemed to her more and more a poor exchange for what they had lost.

"What I find hard to understand is your reaction to this strange event," he went on. "Most people would be up in arms, demanding to know the cause of the explosion, making allegations, demanding protection. Some of your neighbors have even wondered if the whole street should be evacuated as a precaution. You, on the other hand, just accept it. Does that not seem odd?"

"Many people," said Matthew, "would be stunned into silence. It happened in *our* back garden. We were the first to see the hole in the ground. It is not an everyday event."

"Our neighbors," said Alison sharply, "are not worried about a missing daughter, whom the police have done little to find."

The inspector had a yawn. It had been a long day. He did not like these incomprehensible people. He hated this incomprehensible situation.

"That is my main concern," he said coldly. "Despite our best efforts, we have found no trace of Nesta. It seems at least possible that you know more about her disappearance than you care to say. I am not even sure whether there could be some connection between your daughter and this bizarre explosion, or whatever it was. Coincidence is much rarer than you might think."

"I don't know what to say to that," said Matthew. The hairs prickled on the back of his neck as it dawned on him that this man thought that Nesta might have died at the hands of her own parents. What other interpretation could an intelligent listener put on his words?

"Say nothing," said the inspector. "Tomorrow will do. What has happened here tonight is very strange and could be dangerous. We don't know, do we? For tonight, for your protection as much as anything, I would like an officer to remain on the premises. I shall be here myself at nine o'clock in the morning. We can talk further then."

The Gwynns made no protest. They had far too much to hide. But that was only part of it: the events of the night had been stunning, distressing in the extreme. And their daughter was still missing.

The officer, a dour young man in his late twenties, came in and settled himself down in the sitting room.

"We are going to bed now, Constable," said Alison, glaring at him. "There is no point in us sitting here for the rest of the night."

On her way out of the room, she surreptitiously unplugged the telephone. If there were any incoming calls, the phone must ring upstairs, not down. She could not risk her daughter's call being answered by a stranger. By the time she and Matthew were settled in their own room, it was already five past three.

"I won't sleep," said Alison. "She could ring anytime."

She did not know, of course, about the call they had already missed.

# CHAPTER 37

# News and Intrigue

The phone rang in the Gwynn house for the second time that night.

This time the call was successful. Matthew picked up the receiver. Alison was in the bathroom, running a bath. The police constable was downstairs dozing.

"Nesta?" said Matthew eagerly. The one thing that could ease the pain of losing Ormingat would be to hear his daughter speaking to him and assuring him that she was safe.

"Is that Mr. Gwynn?" said the voice at the other end.

"Yes," he replied. "Yes, and who are you?"

His eyes began to gather human tears and his very human heart felt near breaking. All of his emotions were suddenly in conflict. *Ormingat, oh, Ormingat!*

"Are you alone?" said the voice, a woman's voice,

sounding cautious rather than threatening. "No policemen there?"

"Not here in this room," said Matthew. Now Alison was at his shoulder, waiting anxiously to know who was speaking. "There's only myself and my wife."

"So no one else can hear me?" the voice insisted.

"What is it, Mattie?" said Alison impatiently. "Who are you talking to?"

"I don't know yet," said Matthew. "She hasn't said. She just wants to know that no one else can hear us."

Alison put out her hand for the phone and Matthew allowed her to take it.

"Who *are* you?" she said firmly. "And what do you want?"

"Mrs. Gwynn?" said the voice.

"Yes," said Alison. "Now please tell me who you are and why you are ringing here at this time in the morning."

"I am sorry, Mrs. Gwynn," said Stella, "but for all our sakes I have to be careful. The first thing I want you to know is that Nesta is safe and sound and will be traveling home at first light. I shall bring her myself. You will know my name. I am Stella Dalrymple."

"From the newspaper?" said Alison, not quite able to focus on Stella's words.

Matthew gave his wife a look of panic and put a finger to his lips. What could "from the newspaper" mean if not reporters looking for a story?

241

"It's Stella Dalrymple," said his wife. "You remember. She was in that newspaper story, the woman who lived next door to the Derwents and who seemed to know something she wasn't telling. She says she's got Nesta and will be bringing her home in the morning."

Matthew took the receiver and said, "Is this the truth? Are you really Mrs. Dalrymple?"

"I am," said Stella. "And Nesta is asleep in my spare bedroom. She arrived here last night, totally worn out and anxious to come home to you."

"Let me speak to her," said her father.

"I'll waken her shortly," said Stella. "She really is fast asleep. She was exhausted. I promised her I'd contact you after two o'clock. I tried. I let the phone ring for ten minutes but there was no answer. I didn't know what to think. It seemed impossible that you wouldn't be there."

"What has my daughter been telling you?" said Matthew. Why had she waited to ring them till after two o'clock? What reason could Nesta have given to extract this promise from her?

"She told me everything, Mr. Gwynn," said Stella. "She trusts me. She knows that I have known secrets and kept them, secrets almost too fantastic to believe."

"But you believed?" said Matthew.

"What did she believe?" said Alison, taking the receiver again. "Where is my daughter? Is she in

Belthorp? That's where you live, isn't it? But that's miles from here."

"She came by train," said Stella. "We'll come back by train. I'll have her home in York by two in the afternoon. We might have been earlier if it hadn't been Sunday."

"We'll drive up for her," said Alison. "That will be quicker. We'll come straightaway now."

"No," said Stella. "Don't do that. I have had much more time to think about this than you have. No one must ever know where Nesta has been. No one must ever connect you with me."

"Why ever not?" said Alison, still not understanding.

"Your life could be a misery," said Stella. "A man from some ministry or other, some sort of secret service, has already questioned me about Thomas Derwent and his father. If they know that you know me, you will have no peace."

Alison blanched as she thought of the frog that had been slung over their roof with such force. A man "from some ministry" would have a field day!

"It is their job to investigate possible extraterrestrial visitors," said Stella, using the word for the very first time. The cards were all on the table. Nothing was hidden now.

"You will bring her home?" said Alison, skipping any further questions.

"She will be on the platform at York station when the twelve-fifteen arrives from Casselton. I shall escort her all the way, but I shan't leave the train with her. I can't stress how important it is not to tell anyone exactly where she has been."

"The police will ask her questions," said Alison. "They're bound to."

"Parry them," said Stella. "Do whatever you can to fend off the questions and to insist on a return to normal life."

"Can you wake up my daughter now?" said Alison. "I need to hear her voice."

"Of course you do," said Stella gently. "I'll fetch her."

"Mom, oh, Mom," Nesta sobbed into the phone. "I do love you and I am very, very sorry. Stella will bring me home. Let me speak to Dad."

Alison handed the receiver to Matthew.

"Nesta, sweetheart," he said.

"Thanks for not going," said Nesta. "Thanks for staying here on Earth for me, Dad. I love you very much."

She sounded very tired.

"Don't worry," said her father. "In a few hours we'll all be together again. Go back to bed, honey. Have a good sleep."

"We'll have to tell that policeman downstairs that Nesta has been found," said Alison anxiously. "It's hard to know what to say."

"Leave that to me," said Matthew. "I'll say she has rung us and that she is on her way home. They need know nothing more."

"On her way home?" said Detective Inspector Stirling grumpily when he was woken up to be told the latest development. "Where from?"

"They don't know," said the constable awkwardly. Alison and Matthew were standing beside him. He was using the phone in the sitting room, which Alison had discreetly replugged.

"When do they expect her to arrive?"

"They say they are going to meet her at the railway station at two o'clock in the afternoon."

"Oh, oh, oh," said the inspector, fully awake now. "We can't have that. They could be going anywhere. The girl might not even have rung them. She might not be in any state to ring them. Did you hear the phone?"

"No," said the constable, "they were speaking on the line upstairs."

"Let me speak to Mr. Gwynn," said the inspector.

The constable handed the receiver to Matthew.

"Yes?" said Matthew.

"I'll be at your house by eleven in the morning, Mr. Gwynn," said the inspector. "In the meantime, don't go out at all, not even into the garden—forensic will be working there. Make no phone calls. And allow

Constable Bainbridge to answer any incoming calls. We must be very cautious. You do understand?"

"Yes," said Matthew wearily, "you have made yourself perfectly clear." He would have said more, but now was not the time for indignation. Nesta was coming home.

"Now I need to talk to my constable," said the inspector.

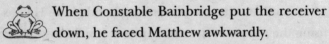 When Constable Bainbridge put the receiver down, he faced Matthew awkwardly.

"I'll have to remove the telephone from your bedroom, sir," he said.

Matthew gave a smile that was half grimace. In a quiet, caustic voice he said, "We haven't murdered our daughter. They won't find her remains buried in the garden."

The constable blushed. But he had his duty to do.

"So can I have the telephone from the bedroom, sir?" he said.

"I'll fetch it down for you," said Matthew.

Constable Bainbridge swallowed audibly.

"I think I am meant to come up and get it, sir. He's bound to ask if I did."

"All right," said Matthew, reluctantly sympathizing with the young man's difficulties. "My daughter is safe and she's coming home. Set beside that, your inspector is a minor irritation."

# CHAPTER 38

# Sunday Morning

Mickey knocked at the door of number 12 Merrivale and rehearsed what he was about to say. It seemed necessary to say it quickly.

"Hello," said Stella, "I was hoping you would call."

"That girl," said Mickey, without a good morning, "she's run away from home and she was on the telly last night—her photo—and her name's Nesta and the police are looking for her."

Stella smiled.

"Come in, Mickey," she said. "Keep calm!"

Mickey said no more but followed her into the house.

The girl was sitting at the dining table. She was just finishing her breakfast. She gave Mickey a shy smile, and then looked at Stella as if expecting a cue. The

247

scene was set but she didn't quite know her lines. What was she going to tell Thomas's friend?

"Nesta is going home this morning," said Stella. "We're going for the train in an hour's time. So there's no need to worry, Mickey. I am going with her all the way to York. I'd ask you to come, but I doubt if your mam would let you."

This was part of a standing joke: Mrs. Trent had reluctantly allowed her son to accompany Mrs. Dalrymple to Casselton when Thomas was in hospital there. It was an occasion he would never be allowed to forget! Mrs. Trent, as they say nowadays, could worry for England! Her son was developing some of the same qualities.

"I'm glad," said Mickey. "Your mam will be happy to have you home again."

It was not the right thing to say. Nesta's eyes filled with tears. She took a wedge of toast from the rack and concentrated upon eating it.

"Sit down and have a cup of tea, Mickey," said Stella, "or you can have chocolate, if you'd rather."

Mickey sat opposite Nesta and said, "I'll have tea, please."

"Do you really know Thomas?" he said, looking directly at Nesta as Stella poured the tea.

"No," said Nesta. "I've never met him. I just know something about him."

It was perhaps less than good-mannered, but there was a question he just had to ask. He had found this girl on the bench by the Green, not knowing where to go or what to do. She had come looking for Mrs. Dalrymple and she claimed to know something about Thomas. That was his excuse and his reason.

"Why did you come all this way to see Mrs. Dalrymple? What do you know about Thomas?"

Nesta looked at Stella, appealing to her to provide the answers.

Stella handed Mickey his tea and offered him toast and jam.

"Nesta had a sort of bad dream," she said in a measured way. "She thought her parents were going to take her in a spaceship no bigger than a golf ball and fly off with her to a distant planet. It was so real she believed it, and she thought it was somehow related to the disappearance of Thomas. It was something she had read about in the newspaper. Stories like that can produce very vivid dreams."

This was a sort of code they had developed to talk in whenever they spoke of anything to do with the Derwents. It seemed wise not to openly admit what they believed, but each knew what the other meant. Mickey nodded.

"It was just a bad nightmare," said Stella.

"A terrible nightmare," said Nesta, shuddering.

Mickey was satisfied now that he knew all that he would ever know about Nesta, and that included the conviction that she too was connected in some way with Ormingat. He felt a sneeze coming on and hastily took out his handkerchief.

"I'm sorry," he said. "I haven't got cold. It is just some sort of allergy. My mam took me to the doctor's about it. He says I'll grow out of it."

Stella smiled.

"I'd better be going now," said Mickey. "I just thought I'd call to see if you were all right after yesterday. I'm going across to Swanson's now for me mam's Sunday paper."

He got up to go.

Nesta said, "Bye, I don't suppose we'll ever see each other again, but thank you for looking after me last night. I felt really lost. I don't know what I'd have done if you hadn't stopped to help me."

"It was nothing," said Mickey with a self-conscious shrug. "And it turned out all right, didn't it?"

At the front door, Stella took Mickey's arm and made him turn to look at her.

"There is one thing you must remember, Mickey," she said. "Don't mention Nesta to anybody, not even your mam. It is best if we forget that she ever came here. Most people wouldn't believe anything about her nightmare; but there are some who might. There are some who would want to prod and probe. The last thing *we* want is for that poor girl to be questioned by Rupert Shawcross or any of his sort."

At nine-thirty Stella and Nesta went to the bus stop just outside the post office. The local bus arrived spot on time, a good thing on a cold morning. There were only the two short stops from there to the station, and then it would hopefully be goodbye, Belthorp.

Nesta enjoyed the ride this time, looking out the bus window through the trees that lined the road, across to sloping fields and distant farmhouses. The bus soon reached the station. Stella and Nesta were the only passengers who got off there. The bus was always quiet on a Sunday morning.

Stella purchased tickets for Casselton from the machine on the platform. The station was empty except for one woman who was about to cross the bridge to take the train going west when she saw Stella and Nesta. She knew Mrs. Dalrymple and stopped to pass the time of day with her.

"Relation?" she said, nodding toward Nesta.

"Distant," said Stella. "She's on her way home to Casselton now."

It was not the truth, but as near as Mary Budd was going to get, and as near as she wanted. It was, after all, just passing the time of day.

"Trains'll be running late today, like as not," said

Mary. "I'm off to see me brother. I hope I don't meet meself coming back!"

Stella just stopped herself from saying, "I hope we don't miss our connection." That was the worst of being a less than skillful liar! No one from the village must know where they were going. She really would have to be very, very careful. The thought of Rupert Shawcross so haunted her that she found herself looking along the empty platform and hoping that he would not suddenly stroll toward them.

The station had a sad winter look about it. The metal bridge that spanned the line was in need of a coat of paint. The sun was at the wrong angle to give any cheer. The waiting room was scruffy and neglected; its little fireplace with the marble mantelpiece was boarded up and painted all over a dull shade of turquoise.

"We'll just wait out here," said Stella, glancing briefly through the waiting room window. "I can remember a time when there would have been a fire in that grate and a stationmaster to attend it. Now it could be part of a ghost town."

But there *was* someone in the waiting room and it wasn't a ghost. A man was sitting there unnoticed, in one corner, arms folded across his chest to keep warm. Suddenly he glanced down at his watch. The train was about due. He stood up, grasped the case he was carrying, and hurried out onto the platform.

Stella was startled as she heard him come up behind her. She turned round abruptly, ready to face the enemy. If it was Rupert Shawcross, she would have to tell whatever lies were needed.

Nesta also turned and, seeing the man, she gasped.

He stood there looking quizzically at the two of them. He had on a long overcoat. Round his neck was a white silk scarf, fringed with tassels. His face was dark, his eyes deep brown and twinkling. His smile showed a row of very white teeth. He was the man who had so frightened Nesta the night before.

"Oh, Mr. Montori!" said Stella. "How you startled me!"

"I seem to have developed the habit of startling people!" he said with a laugh, and he stretched out one hand and ruffled Nesta's hair. "Nice to see you, though. Now I must get across the bridge before my train comes in."

Stella and Nesta watched him walk away. He flung one end of the scarf across his shoulder and went off whistling. He was carrying a cello case.

"Nice man," said Stella. "Very gifted. The whole family is."

Nesta blushed and said nothing. That moment of fear was the one thing she had not told Stella. It had seemed too foolish.

The train on the other side of the platform came in first. Stella and Nesta had to wait another ten minutes for theirs. By the time it came, they were shivering with cold and very grateful to get aboard and find a seat.

As the train rolled out of the station, Stella grasped Nesta's hand and said, "Well, we're on the move now. It won't be long before you're home."

# CHAPTER 39

# Detective Inspector Stirling Returns

The people of Linden Drive had returned to privacy after the rumpus of the night before. Some still peeped from behind leaded lights and vertical blinds to watch the comings and goings around number 8. The day was as cold as ever, but the sun was shining brightly.

Each household had its own theory as to what had occurred.

"Methane gas—bet you what you like."

"Terrorists? Couldn't be—not in *this* street!"

"A store of fireworks exploding? Used to be just Guy Fawkes, but they have the darned things all year round now."

"An unexploded bomb left over from the war? If it's that it'll be on the news—we'd better watch it tonight."

Out in the street, a coven of cones had gathered round the holes in the road. A large yellow van was parked outside number 16. To the other side of the damaged area was a council wagon, and across the road a still and silent police car. This was Sunday morning in suburbia: work on the holes would not begin till Monday. The water main had been made safe. The only real activity was in the back garden of number 8, where two workmen and a presiding scientist were digging out and inspecting what was left of the lily pad.

"Found anything?" said Inspector Stirling. He had come straight round to the back of the house on arrival.

"Nothing so far," said the boffin from the lab. He was tired and yawning and in no mood for probing questions.

"No sign of a detonator, or some such device?" persisted the inspector. He stepped down into the basin of the pond.

Cayley, the lab man, suppressed a smile as he said, "All we've found is this."

He stooped and turned something. Water immediately sprayed into the air, sprinkling the inspector so that he had to jump back on the grass.

"It's for filling the pond," said Cayley innocently. "As you see, it is not even broken, though the nozzle should be set at a lower angle, I suppose."

Inspector Stirling glared at him as he made angry swipes at his damp jacket with his pocket handkerchief. He had really thought there might be some sign of a child's clothing, if nothing more gory. It was not that he relished the thought of infanticide; it was more that his suspicions now were so strong that it would have been a relief to have some sort of confirmation.

"We may have to dig up the whole garden eventually," he said. There was no doubt in his mind that the visit to York station would draw a blank. However many people might step off the train, Nesta Gwynn would not be one of them.

After that, he said no more and strode round the side of the house to the front door, where his constable was already waiting for him.

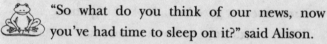 "So what do you think of our news, now you've had time to sleep on it?" said Alison.

"I'll be able to tell you that when we've met your daughter at the station. You say she is on her way home, but we have no proof of that, do we?" said the inspector. Then he added abruptly, "And where is she on her way from?"

"We don't know," said Matthew. "She hung up without saying."

"You must know which train you are meant to be meeting," said the inspector.

"I see what you mean," said Matthew. "We hadn't

257

thought of that. She said she'd be on the London train. So she must be coming from somewhere north of here, though that doesn't tell us very much. It could be anywhere between here and Edinburgh, I suppose."

"Well, we'll see, shan't we?" said Stirling, his cold, fish eyes fixed on a spot somewhere behind the Gwynns. They were all standing in the front room. Outside the window, the yellow van moved off noisily, its work done for the day.

"I shall accompany you, of course," the inspector added in a soft voice, with a false smile. "It might be a good idea if we all traveled in my car."

"No," said Alison, glaring at him. "We shall take our own car. You can follow us. I have never traveled in a police vehicle, and I don't intend to do so now."

The inspector gave her a look of impatience.

"Then I shall have to travel in *your* car," he said.

"Is that not extreme?" said Matthew. "What do you think we are going to do? Have a car chase through York? Make a dash for the nearest airport?"

"I never think too far ahead," said the inspector. "After all, it was you who asked us to find your daughter. I would like to accompany you to the station and be there when she alights from the train. That seems to me only right and fitting."

The Gwynns both shrugged. The inspector's damp clothing on a dry though cold morning might have made them wonder, but they said nothing. The inspector himself totally ignored the splashes the pond pump had made. An automaton could not have been more impervious.

"It is now eleven-forty-five. Be ready to go in an hour. I'll come back for you. P. C. Bainbridge will go off duty now. Another constable is waiting to take over. I know this may seem unwarranted to you, but it is purely and simply a safety measure."

Then, with the abruptness that was ingrained in him, he left the room and the house without any farewell.

As the door closed behind him, Alison gave it a look full of fury.

"Don't let him get to you," said Matthew, seeing her clenched fists and taut face.

"If only Nesta had agreed to go to Ormingat," she said, "none of this would have happened."

"If only," echoed Matthew with a deep sigh. "We would be on our way home by now! But regrets are just as useless as anger. It's no good crying over spilt milk. We are now permanent, lifelong citizens of Earth. Whatever powers we have had will fade away. I can feel myself already losing the reality of Ormingat; even its name is changing on my tongue. Though I can't think that the sense of loss will ever leave me. There will always be an emptiness."

Alison clutched his hand in comfort. She felt,

almost guiltily, that his feeling of desolation was somehow greater than hers.

"Let's have something for lunch," said Matthew, squeezing the hand that held his. They would always have each other, and would never be lacking in loving kindness. "It will pass the time. Besides, I'm hungry!"

Their new policeman came in and conscientiously followed them into the kitchen. He was clearly embarrassed but, like his predecessor, he obeyed orders. He was very young and quite slightly built, not the stuff that bodyguards are made of!

"I'm making some tuna sandwiches, Constable," said Alison as she reached up into the cupboard for a tin of fish, "nothing ambitious or likely to blow up. Perhaps you would like some?"

The constable coughed awkwardly before saying, "No thank you, Mrs. Gwynn. I've already eaten."

"Coffee, then?" she said. "Surely your inspector won't mind if you have a cup of coffee with the suspects. Though I shudder to think what he suspects us of."

"Leave the lad alone, Alison," said Matthew. "You can see how embarrassed he is. None of this is his fault. We know we have done no wrong, and we know we have cause to celebrate. An hour from now we'll be on our way home with our daughter."

"I *will* have that cup of coffee," said the young man

quite suddenly. "And I'm glad your daughter's safe and well."

He had a right to his own opinion, after all, and he felt happy to express it, even though in this story he is a man without a name.

# CHAPTER 40

# The Journey Home

The train left Belthorp station at eleven-twenty-five. It consisted of only two carriages. Even so, it was almost empty.

Stella gave Nesta the window seat and for a while they traveled in silence, neither quite knowing what to say. Fields passed, sloping up from the railway cutting. Then on the horizon they saw a stone-built farmhouse.

"I often think," said Stella, "when I pass a house like that, all on its own, that inside there are people living lives I'll never know anything about. I won't even know their name. The world is a very private place, unless you are famous."

"Would you like to be famous?" said Nesta.

"Probably not," said Stella, smiling. "I suppose it would depend upon what I was famous for. Mostly people are happier getting on with their lives and remaining anonymous."

"You weren't anonymous when that article was in the paper."

"No, I wasn't," said Stella ruefully. "I was asked lots of questions by people I didn't really take to. *You* will be asked questions when you get home. My guess is that the police will want to know where you have been, not just your parents. So listen to me very carefully. You must say nothing about knowing me. No connection must be made between Thomas Derwent and yourself. I am the only link. If you are stuck for an answer, refuse to speak. Your mum and dad will back you up. They have a secret they wish to share with nobody on Earth. You must help guard that secret."

"I told *you* the secret," said Nesta, shamefaced.

"You didn't. You couldn't tell me what I knew already. I loved the family that came to me from Ormingat. That alone is enough to ensure my silence."

Nesta looked at her in puzzlement.

"Are you not curious? I mean, do you not wonder?" she said, not quite knowing how to put the question. But Stella knew, and Stella knew the answer.

"We are all visitors to this Earth," she said. "We won't any of us live here forever. I can be filled with amazement and find myself puzzling as to what the truth can be. But I don't expect to know all the answers. Sharing my world with Patrick and Thomas was a privilege. Knowing and helping you is another gift of fate."

The train halted at Chamfort. An old man got on and sat in the seat behind them. With a whole carriage to choose from, he decided to sit within hearing distance of two other passengers. At least it felt like hearing distance, and it made Stella and Nesta fall silent again.

At Casselton, Stella bought herself a return ticket for York. Nesta still had her own ticket tucked safely in the pocket of the fleece jacket.

As Stella came away from the ticket office, she suddenly thought of telephoning Nesta's parents again. But then she felt it might not be safe. They knew enough already. Police might be hovering by.

"Can I make a phone call?" said Nesta.

"Better not," said Stella. "Your parents know which train you are on. I'd have phoned them if there had been any complications, but so far so good. We want to take as few risks as possible."

"It's not Mom and Dad I want to phone," said Nesta. "I'd like to ring Amy and tell her I'm on my way back."

"That's not possible either," said Stella. "I know that Amy was good to you, but if you rang her home it is very likely that one of her parents would answer. They would ask questions that might cause trouble for both of you. You'll just have to wait till you're safely back home."

The York train was twenty minutes late, but otherwise the journey from Casselton was uneventful. An unexpected halt south of Darlington set the train back a further twenty minutes.

Nesta looked out of the window anxiously.

"Don't worry," said Stella. "They'll know how late the train is at York. The time goes up on the notice board."

When, at length, the train was about to draw into York station, Stella got up from her seat, bent over, and kissed Nesta's brow and said quietly, "Now I am going along to another carriage. I'll be getting off to take the train back to Casselton, but we must not be seen together. I'll watch from a distance, in case of difficulties. But I am absolutely sure there won't be any."

"Does that mean I'll never see you again?" said Nesta. "I'd love for you to meet my parents. You really have been very good to me."

Stella heard the regret in Nesta's voice. She felt regret herself, even though she had known the girl for such a short time.

"Perhaps we could write to each other," said Nesta.

"For the foreseeable future, even that wouldn't be wise," said Stella. "You have to realize just how dangerous that could be. Take my word for it, there are definitely people on this Earth who would give none of us any peace if they had the slightest suspicion of the truth. I wouldn't want you to have people like Rupert Shawcross pestering you week in week out."

Nesta still looked regretful.

"Maybe someday your parents can take a holiday up north," said Stella as she prepared to walk down the train, "and we can meet, by chance, and become acquainted as if we had never met before. But that couldn't be this year, or even next. The risk is too great."

# CHAPTER 41

# The Last Chapter

On the drive to the station, the Gwynns never spoke. Inspector Stirling sat uncomfortably in the backseat, his long legs and bulky frame unaccustomed to this inferior position in a small car. He was relieved when they crossed Lendal Bridge and turned toward the station.

The Gwynns had allowed themselves ample time to meet the London train, but they found when they got there that there was really no hurry. The train was already running more than half an hour late.

"Would you like coffee?" asked the inspector, anxious to think of some way to pass the time.

"No," said Alison. Not "No thank you," just a crisp, firm "No."

"Shall we sit here then?" said the inspector, indicating one of the benches in the waiting area.

"No, Inspector," said Alison. "You do what you like. I am going to stand on the platform till the train comes in."

The inspector looked at Matthew to check what he would think of standing on a cold platform for thirty minutes or more.

"Agreed," said Matthew without even glancing at the policeman. "Platform three, isn't it? We'll go there now."

It was, in fact, the platform nearest the main hall. A few steps took them onto it. They walked right to the far end, leaving the inspector to follow; which he did, slowly, feeling uncomfortable at following, uninvited and clearly unwanted. They were not making it easy for him!

The Gwynns placed themselves almost on the edge of the concrete, without even a pillar for support. The inspector, scanning the platform, decided it would be safe to sit on the seat directly behind them, which happened to be totally unoccupied, though there were actually four seats in a row all joined together. It was not ideal, but to stand nearer to this close-knit couple, being pointedly ignored by them, was an even more embarrassing option. He needed to move offstage. On other seats, nearer the entrance, passengers of various shapes and sizes sat reading or yawning or clutching their cases. The inspector sat back with his arms folded, never taking his eyes off the suspects. Thank goodness the station wasn't crowded this Sunday lunchtime. Rush hour on a Friday would have made his job impossible.

Suddenly, Matthew moved off to the right, leaving Alison standing alone. The inspector got up, uncertain whether to follow him or to stay with his wife. He approached her fussily.

"Where has your husband gone?" he said.

"In search of a loo," said Alison with a smile that was somewhat malicious. "I told him he should have gone before we came out."

She was almost tempted to do her Mrs. Jolly impression and take the conversation even further, explaining how . . . but she resisted it. Inspector Stirling looked embarrassed. He decided to stand beside Mrs. Gwynn till her husband returned.

In a very short time he was back again.

"The inspector's been worried about you," said Alison in a clear voice. "You should really have put your hand up and asked to leave the room!"

Inspector Stirling, with fair dignity, made no remark and returned to his seat.

Over the tannoy, a voice said boomingly, "The terrain from Edinburgh Waverley, which was scheduled to be arriving at plat-ty-form three, will now arrive at plat-ty-form five. We regret that it is now running forty-five minutes ley-ate. Passengers for London Kings Ca-ross will please go to plat-ty-form five on the other side of the ber-ridge."

Matthew looked at his watch.

"That's another twenty minutes before it gets here," he said. "Let's get to platform five straightaway."

They walked toward the bridge and the inspector followed them.

When they got to the platform, they saw that a man and a boy were sitting on two of the seats immediately below the ramp, both holding in front of them tall bundles of what looked like fishing tackle. Other sets of seats, further along, were totally free. Alison and Matthew smiled at one another and sat down beside the fishermen. The inspector was left either to stand or to look for a vacant seat elsewhere.

*They're playing games,* he thought irritably. *Let's see what sort of a game they'll play when that train comes in without their daughter on board!* He pulled up his over-coat collar, took out his mobile phone, and, as surrep-titiously as possible, rang his driver, who was waiting in the police car outside, having followed them as in-structed from the house in Linden Drive.

"I might need backup," he said. "They're waiting for the London train and I'm sure they know their daugh-ter can't be on it. If they try to board the train, I'll de-tain them. If I buzz you, you'll know they're being difficult. Then you'll leave the car and join me—but let the station know you're doing it. They can send round another car, just in case."

The train came in, at long last. Doors opened. Passengers alighted. And among them, from the carriage marked D, came a slightly built schoolgirl in a red fleece coat and black leggings. For a moment, in the clothes she was wearing, her mother did not recognize her. Then the girl's hand shot up in the air and she waved furiously as she ran toward them.

"Mom! Dad! I'm home!" she yelled, so loudly that other passengers stared at her and were amused.

Nesta rushed into her mother's arms. The excitement turned to tears and she stood there sobbing her heart out. No thought now of Stella Dalrymple or spaceships or distant planets. *My mom, my dad, my home, my world.*

"I am sorry," she said, "really and truly sorry."

"There, there," said Alison, stroking her hair and murmuring softly, as to a hurt baby. *Kiss it better.*

"I know I shouldn't have run away," said Nesta, drawing deep breaths to hold back her sobs. "I just couldn't face . . ."

Her mother clutched her arm urgently. The inspector had come just a little too close.

"What could you not face, Nesta?" he said quickly.

The girl looked sharply at the stranger and clung more closely to her mother.

"This is Inspector Stirling," said Alison, emphasizing the word *inspector*. "He has been helping us to search for you, though none of us knew where to start."

Recalling Stella's words of warning, Nesta turned away, hid her head deeply in her mother's shoulder, and said nothing.

Detective Inspector Stirling, to give him his full title, was about to speak again, to assert his authority, when Matthew looked at him and said gently, for he was a very gentle man, "Leave them, Inspector. This has been an ordeal for both of them—and for me."

Alison looked over Nesta's shoulder at the looming policeman.

"You can go now," she said. "I am sure you can see that my daughter is safe and well."

"But where has she been?" said the inspector, "and why did she go? And what about the frog? Reporters from the local papers have already shown interest. It is not something that will go away."

"The two events were totally unconnected," said Alison icily. "Do what you think best about the explosion in our back garden. Myself, I would put it down to a freak buildup of underground gas. But your scientists might know better. At least you know that you are unlikely to find a dead body there."

Inspector Stirling was not put out by her remarks. He simply ignored them.

"You do see, Mrs. Gwynn, that after four nights' absence from home, it would at least be prudent for us to find the answers to some of our questions. The Social Services will be concerned."

Alison looked up into his pale fish eyes, which lacked any spark of real intelligence: dull-witted and dogged.

"Leave it," said Alison peremptorily. "Go away and leave it. I believe you have a driver waiting in a car outside. You go to your car. We'll go to ours."

Nesta never spoke. She moved from her mother's arms to her father's and silently hugged him. Matthew felt how fragile she was, and he had that fragility to set against his own sense of bereavement. How could she know, or even guess, what pain she had inflicted?

"It's good to have you back," he said softly, so that no one but his daughter heard, "to have you safe home."

The inspector looked at Alison, paused, faltered for a few moments, and then walked obediently away. She had used the power of Ormingat for the very last time. Her subject would know exactly what had occurred, but it would become no more important to him than a snarl-up in the local traffic. Case closed. Pass on the paperwork!

# You'll want to read

Sylvia Waugh

Meet the first travelers from Ormingat to land on Earth.

An ALA Notable Children's Book
A *School Library Journal* Best Book of the Year
A *Horn Book* Fanfare

★ "Readers will enjoy the exciting plot and fast-moving action, and the sympathetic characters will stay with them long after the book is closed."
—*School Library Journal*, Starred

★ "Waugh beams out the message that the driving force in the universe is love—no matter what planet you're from."
—*The Horn Book Magazine*, Starred